A FIGHT FOR FREEDOM

Sundance and Dumont manhandled the cannon around the side of the wagon.

"Get back now," Sundance warned Dumont. "Your people need you more than they need me."

He adjusted the range and elevation. It looked all right, as good as he could make it. A lot of lives were riding on those two shells.

"Now!"

He touched a lighted fuse to the cannon. It dug back on its wooden carriage as the shell screamed straight at the gate of the fort.

There was a splintering crash as some of the thick verticals in the gate gave way. White smoke boiled up from the muzzle of the cannon, and from the *métis* ranks a wild cheer went up.

SUNDANCE

DAY OF THE HALFBREEDS

Peter McCurtin

LEISURE BOOKS • **NEW YORK CITY**

A LEISURE BOOK

Published by

Nordon Publications, Inc.
Two Park Avenue
New York, N.Y. 10016

**DAY OF THE HALFBREEDS is #29 in the
SUNDANCE SERIES.**
Other titles are:

One

"What do you want, halfbreed?"

The challenge was hurled at Jim Sundance by a burly Scotsman in the scarlet coat of the Royal North West Mounted Police. The policeman, wearing sergeant's stripes on his sleeve, made no attempt to hide his hostility. His pale-blue eyes were hard, his meaty face lined with bitterness. As he spoke, he touched the flapped-over holster with his thumb.

It was November 16, 1885, a bright, biting cold morning in Regina, Saskatchewan, and thousands of people had come to witness the hanging of the most loved and hated man in Canada. Louis Riel had finally come to the end of his road; Sundance had come a very long way to see him off.

"I have a pass," Sundance said, handing the paper to the Mountie.

He waited while the sergeant sent a trooper to find a superior officer. Overhead, the sky was a brilliant blue; on the prairie around the raw new frontier town, hoarfrost glittered in the sun.

The double line of militiamen and Mounties stood watching Sundance, for even in the wild North West

Territories—a land of halfbreeds—he was an unusual sight, with his flowing yellow hair and skin the color of an old penny. Tall and lean, he was dressed in buckskins and carried himself with the assurance of a professional fighting man. Hanging from his tooled leather belt were a long-barreled Colt .44, a razor-edged Bowie knife, and a straight-handled throwing hatchet.

"My name is Mackenzie," the Mountie officer said, coming back with the pass in his gloved hand. His wind-burned face was tired, showing the strain of the execution that was to take place in less than an hour. "You'll have to give up your weapons before you can go in. Everybody is on edge. I'll walk along with you in case one of the guards gets nervous."

Sundance nodded. Only eight weeks had passed since Louis Riel had led his army of halfbreeds and Indians against the government of Canada. The whole country was braced for another outbreak of violence. Soldiers from all over Canada had been drafted to the North West Territories, and men slept with guns beside their beds. The cold, clear air crackled with tension.

Mackenzie thumped on the door with his fist, giving the password when it was called for. High up on the stone tower of the jail and police barracks, two Gatling guns were mounted, ready to rake the square with lead as the hour of execution grew closer.

Inside the jail, it was colder than it was outside in the sunshine. An iron-faced door banged open and shut; nail-shod boots echoed in the hallways.

"I've heard of you, Mr. Sundance," Mackenzie said. "It's hard to think that it would come to this. If only Riel hadn't come back. Nobody would ever have bothered him in Montana. But he came back and had to be stopped."

"That's right. He had to be stopped. That won't make his people feel any better after he's dead. It won't make me feel any better."

8

"You think there will be peace now?"

"That's hard to say. Your government has the money and the guns."

"But it's their government too. We couldn't just let Riel start his own country right in the middle of Canada."

Try telling that to the halfbreeds, Sundance thought. He knew what it was like to be a halfbreed, a man caught between the races, belonging no place. Though Louis Riel, madman or patriot (depending on which side you were on), had very little Indian blood, he had fought long and hard for those he considered to be his people.

"Well, he's stopped now," Sundance said with finality, thinking of Louis Riel and John Brown and all the madmen who were ready to die for what they believed was right.

They went up a steel staircase to the third floor of the jail. On the way up, they were stopped twice by heavily armed guards.

"How is he taking it?" Sundance asked.

"You know Riel so you already know the answer," Mackenzie said. "Nothing bothers him. He writes for hours every day. I don't have the heart to tell him that nobody will ever read it. I have strict orders to destroy his papers once he's dead. In time perhaps he'll be forgotten."

Sundance said, "He won't be forgotten. It doesn't matter what you do with his papers; he won't be forgotten. Hanging him will only make it worse."

A guard stood outside the door of Riel's cell. "He's had the priest," he told Mackenzie. "Said he didn't want any breakfast, just coffee. He's still writing in that book of his."

Mackenzie spoke to Sundance. "I can only let you have fifteen minutes. If you don't want to stay that long, bang on the door. After that we'll have to get him ready. You'll be his last visitor except for..."

There was no need to complete the sentence. Riel's last

visitors would be the governor of the jail, the priest—and the hangman.

The door closed behind Sundance and the key turned in the lock. In the cold, narrow stone cell there were few furnishings except for a bunk, a small unpainted table, and a chair. Louis Riel sat at the table beneath the barred window set high in the wall. A big silver watch lay on the table beside the inkwell; the only sound was the hurried scratching of his pen.

"Is that you, Mr. Mackenzie?" Riel asked without turning his head. The pen raced on across the paper. "Surely, it isn't time yet?"

"Not yet, Louis," Sundance said quietly.

A smile spread across Riel's dark, brooding face as he stood up quickly and extended his hand. "Jim Sundance, you came all this way. I hoped you would come, but your letters were written from so far away. Do you want some coffee? It's still hot."

Sundance sat on the edge of the bunk. "I did the best I could, Louis. So did General Crook. He wrote to the President and everybody else he could think of. It didn't do any good. I'm sorry."

Riel handed Sundance a tin cup of black coffee. "No need to be sorry. I knew what I was doing all the time. I don't even blame Macdonald. He let me escape to Montana the first time. But what good would I be as a schoolteacher in Montana? Every day I was there I thought of nothing but my people, what was happening to them in the Territories. It wasn't getting better, Jim, it was getting worse. I knew I could never call myself a man if I didn't come back."

"And here you are, Louis."

Riel's English was fluent with only a trace of a French-Canadian accent. "You're taking it worse than I am. Don't you see? There are some things that can't be changed. All my life, during all my wanderings, I knew—I *knew* that this was how it had to end. But oh what a fight we gave them, Louis Riel and his *métis*! It took nearly ten-thousand of them to do it. We might even have won if they didn't have the railroad. Perhaps not won great battles, but concessions. We might have forced them to let us live in peace on the land of our fathers. You would have thought that Canada was big enough for all of us—such a vast country stretching away to the end of the world!"

"You won some things, Louis," Sundance said. "Not your own country, but many things. From now on, they'll always know they can't push people too far."

Riel nodded in agreement. "What you say is true. But what a country we could have had! Free from the stink of factories and cities! To trap and fish and hunt the buffalo."

"The buffalo is almost gone, Louis."

"We could have brought them back. That was one of the plans of my government. We could have made the Red River into a land of plenty. It could have become truly the land of free men without interference from the fatted politicians in Ottawa. There would be towns but no cities. The English and the Scotch would have been welcome there but not as speculators and and money-grubbers. The Red River settlements would have been as example to all freedom-loving peoples."

"There can still be freedom, Louis. Not exactly as you saw it, but your fight hasn't been for nothing. In your forty years you have accomplished many things."

Riel said, "If I had another forty, even another ten, I could remake this country. I have been called a madman because of what I tried to do. But if you don't burn hotly, you soon flicker out. I have seen it happen to other men with a special view of what life should be. Do you think I'm a madman, Jim?"

"I have considered the idea from time to time. I'd be a liar if I said I didn't."

11

Riel glanced at his watch and laughed. "That's one thing you'll never be. You told me what to expect if I went ahead with my plans. I knew you were right in many ways, but there was nothing I could do. My people needed a leader, and I was that leader. There is no boast in what I say, simply fact. If there had been a stronger leader, I would have stepped aside in his favor. People have never believed that, yet it's the truth. My people are brave, but they have lived all their lives on the prairies. Bravery isn't always enough, not when you are faced with Maxim guns and railroads and modern armies. I was the only leader who could bring their plight to the attention of the world. In the great cities—New York, London, Paris—they know who we are and what we tried to do here in the wilderness."

"They know all right," Sundance said. "There isn't an important newspaper in the world that hasn't carried the news. Right now, thousands of people are marching in Montreal and all over France."

"Good! Good!" Riel said.

Sundance said, "Will there be trouble in the Territories today? There has been talk."

"You mean more bloodshed?"

"There is talk of that, Louis. There is still time to stop it. Your people wouldn't have a chance. The militia would crush them in days. They'd drive them out onto the prairies and hunt them down to the last man. With winter coming on, no food . . . you know the rest."

"There won't be any more trouble, Jim. I could have escaped after that last battle. I stayed and let them capture me because I knew the Canadian government would be looking for a victim. Give me any name you like. I stayed so the politicians in Ottawa could take out their anger on me. You know what Macdonald said during the riots that followed my conviction for treason? 'Riel shall hang even if every dog in Quebec barks in his favor.'"

"I read that," Sundance said.

"That's how the English think of us—as dogs," Riel said. "But we bit them hard enough. You can kick a dog for just so long, then he shows his teeth."

Riel looked at this watch and smoothed back his long black hair with his fingers. His crow-black hair was the only sign of his Indian blood.

"They'll be coming in a few minutes," he said. "Don't ever blame yourself for the part you had in this."

"Maybe I should have stayed out of it."

"Nothing would have changed. You can be certain of that. Don't get discouraged because of what happened here. Continue to fight for the Indians, as you have always done. Your enemies in Washington may get you in the end, but don't ever give up. Ah yes, my friends are coming up the stairs to get me. You will walk down to the second floor with me? That's where the end comes for Louis Riel. Don't forget me, Jim."

"I would never do that, Louis."

Mackenzie came into the cell followed by the others. The hangman, a short fat man in his sixties, stood to one side while the priest offered up prayers for the dead in a loud voice.

"It's time to go," Mackenzie said.

Two

Nearly a year before, Sundance had been in Fort Riley, Kansas, when a telegram arrived from General George Crook, now commander of the Department of the Missouri, with headquarters in Chicago. There was no explanation because, between Sundance and his old friend George Crook, none was necessary. The message asked him to come to Chicago as soon as he could. Sundance was on the next available train.

The two men, halfbreed and major general in the United States Army, had been close friends for many years. They had campaigned together in the wars against Geronimo and again later on the high plains. Sundance had served under Crook as scout and hunter. Between them, there was a bond that could never be broken. When there were no wars to be fought, and when their paths happened to cross, they hunted and fished together. Crook was a no-nonsense veteran, liked by his men and respected by the Indians he had fought so long and so hard. Liquor and foul language had no place in his life, but he smoked one black cigar after another, despite the warnings of his wife and doctor. There was nothing Sundance would not have done for George Crook.

Sundance got Eagle from the box-car in which the great fighting stallion had traveled from Kansas. "Easy boy!" he said as his horse whickered nervously at the crash and roar of the city. It had been years since Sundance had been in Chicago, and he didn't like it any better now. He didn't like cities of any kind, and Chicago was one of the noisiest of them all.

It took him an hour to ride across town and find General Crook's headquarters in the newly built military reservation. It was winter. Dirty, frozen snow was on the ground and a vicious wind was blowing in from the lake. A sentry passed him through the gate and a corporal escorted him to Crook's office. He had to wait for five minutes before the general came out to greet him. A white-haired man in a gray broadcloth suit stared at Sundance as he left the room. Sundance thought he looked familiar, a face from the newspapers.

"Did you ever see such weather?" Crook said. "Lord, how I'd like to be back in Arizona. I wonder if it's true that the desert makes a man's blood thin. Come on in by the fire and get warm. I'll shout up some coffee for both of us."

A stack of logs burned in the fireplace with a cheerful crackle. "Sit down, Jim," Crook said, rubbing his large hands together. "I tell you, this new job of mine doesn't suit me at all—shuffling papers all day. You get worse saddle sores from sitting in a chair than you ever got from any saddle. I only took the job to please Mary. We're both not so young anymore, and she thought it was time we settled down to a more civilized existence. Damnation! I'd go back to sleeping in a tent any time."

Sundance smiled at the general. "You'll get the hang of it after a while."

"Absolutely not," Crook said. "I'm a fighting soldier and always was, from the first day I left the Point. Mary is fine by the way."

15

An orderly brought in a pot of coffee and Sundance waited while Crook poured.

Back behind his desk with a cup in one hand and a cigar in the other, Crook said, "I guess you're wondering why I sent for you, Jim. I couldn't explain in the telegram because it would take too long. Besides, too many people in and out of the army have long noses. This isn't like anything I've asked you to do before, so you're free to turn it down. I'll understand if you do."

"It isn't likely that I will, Three Stars," Sundance said, using the old Cheyenne name for General Crook. The general was known to his men as Old George; to Sundance he would always be Three Stars.

"Hear me out first," Crook said. "The whole thing is about as complicated as it can get. You know there are people in this country who would like to annex or steal Canada. Yes, sir, we have people with mighty big ideas in the U.S.A. From sea to shining sea isn't big enough for them. Now it has to be Canada, the whole Dominion. 'Manifest destiny' is the fancy name they give it. Of course, it's just another name for some plain and fancy stealing. But that's politics for you. No matter how fat a politician gets, he wants to get fatter. It's the nature of the beast."

Sundance drank his coffee. It was army coffee, which was all you could say for it.

Crook went on: "Not every politician in Washington is in favor of annexation. But lot of them are. So are their friends in business, who lick their lips every time they think of that big rich mostly empty country up there—mining, lumber, furs, millions of acres of some of the finest land in the world, all waiting to be stolen by Uncle Sam."

"What about the British," Sundance asked. "They're not known to take these things lying down."

Crook said, "I was coming to that. Some people in our

16

government are convinced the British will fight if it comes to a showdown. Others aren't so sure. Their argument is that Great Britain is thousands of miles away. Ever since the Civil War, this country has one of the most powerful armies in the world. Britain, they argue, isn't about to get into a major war over a wilderness like Canada."

"What do you think?"

"I honestly don't know. They're a tough people, the British, and they may see it as a matter of pride. I'd hate to see Washington shelled all over again, not to mention Boston and New York. I'm inclined to think they'll fight. That's only one man's opinion, and there are men, men I respect, who don't agree with me. Lord, I'd hate to see a war with England. But that's only part of the problem. It gets worse as it goes along. You ever hear of a man named Louis Riel?"

"The so-called halfbreed leader?"

"That's the one. How much do you know about him?"

"That he started a halfbreed rebellion in the North West Territories about fifteen years ago, was defeated, and managed to escape to Montana."

Crook said, "He didn't manage to escape. They let him escape to keep him from becoming a martyr. A lot of people wanted to see him hung, but they let him escape instead. For fifteen years he stayed in Montana, taught school, and wrote a lot of fiery speeches, and not much else was heard from him. Now he's back in the North West Territories threatening to establish a separate government dominated by halfbreeds and Indians. If the movement goes far enough, there is going to be a bloody war up there."

"I thought the Territories belonged to the Hudson Bay Company."

"Not for much longer. The company no longer has effective control over the area and is turning it over to the Canadian government. The transfer hasn't been made yet, so there is nobody in real control. That's why Riel is trying to seize control—when the situation is confused. He tried it once before, but now he has a better chance."

"Because he has outside help from this country?"

"How did you know?"

"Just a guess. Now would be the time to look for help."

"And get it," Crook said, "from the politicians and the business men. The Irish don't want to be left out either. By Irish I mean the Fenians. Any trouble that can be made for England, the Fenians are ready to take part in it. You remember the time they tried to invade Canada after the Civil War? They were beaten off by the militia and some British regulars. Now they're looking for another chance. They've been collecting money and recruiting men in New York, Boston, and even right here in Chicago. Our government isn't doing much to stop them. There's that monster of all northern politicians, the Irish vote."

Sundance said, "All the halfbreeds and Indians will suffer while the others look after their own interests."

"Riel doesn't think so. That's the information I have. Riel thinks he can handle all of them when the time comes. Look, Jim, I don't say the halfbreeds and Indians don't have just complaint. They've lived up there in the Territories for as long as man can remember. Suddenly, the Canadian government is interested in their lands, wants them to prove their titles. What do these poor people know about land titles? It's their land because they have always lived there. Now they're being trod underfoot by government surveyors. It all sounds reasonable on paper, but these people live with the hard facts of life, not scraps of paper. It's a desperate situation, and Riel is playing into the hands of men who are no friends of his people."

Sundance had been thinking of Louis Riel. That the man was a fanatic there was no doubt. But then, so were all desperate men. A halfbreed himself, he could well

18

understand Riel's despair. Governments promised much and did nothing until desperate men broke out their guns.

"You haven't come to the worst part yet," he suggested to General Crook.

"God help me, I haven't, Jim. Riel has very little Indian blood, perhaps none, but the halfbreeds and Indians—the Crees—look up to him. They fought with him in the first rebellion and will fight harder now. Riel's plan is to call for a general uprising of all the Indian tribes on both sides of the border—all the tribes. And he thinks he can do it. If that happens, the frontier will be washed in blood. It will make all the Indian wars of the past look like skirmishes."

"Has he white support in this, Three Stars?"

"My information is that he does. It will give our government an excuse to invade Canada, to crush Riel, and scatter his forces. Once we're in, we'll want to stay to make sure of a lasting peace. The President doesn't want that to happen, but there won't be much he can do about it. There will be so much flagwaving he wouldn't even try—not and stay in office, that is. I tell you, Jim, this business scares the dickens out of me."

"How many people know about it?"

"No way to be sure. Plenty of people know about it but are afraid to take sides. They'd like to sit out the dance and perhaps make a little money when the slaughter is over. Sumner and Seward started it. They've always had their eyes on Canada. They liked to pretend it was because Canada harbored Rebels during the Civil War. Not so. They just want to steal the country."

"What about the army?"

"The high-ranking officers know about it, or have heard something. Some don't believe it because this annex Canada talk has been going on for years. It goes clear back to the Revolutionary War. Some officers would like to see another war. Nothing like a war for quick promotion. I've known too many men who have built their careers on the bones of others."

"Three Stars, what would you like me to do? What do you think I *could* do? You just drew a dismal picture."

Crook got up and walked around, angry and glum at the same time.

"I'll be blunt. You're a halfbreed and know how it feels to be treated like one. I don't say anyone has done that lately, but you were once a boy. You saw the scorn heaped on your parents. With you it isn't something learned from a book. Do you think Louis Riel knows who you are?"

"It's possible. I've been in Canada. My name has been in the newspapers, though not as often in Canada as here."

"Do you think Riel would listen to you? If you went north and explained what I have told you? I'm told those blamed Fenians, those Irishmen, are already with him. Their leader is a man named Colum Hardesty. He's thirty-eight or forty and served in the British army before landing in New York ten years ago. Hardesty has two friends, named Cunningham and Lane. It would be a shame if something happened to them."

Crook stared out the window and bit the end off another cigar. "If you know what I mean."

"I could try talking to Riel," Sundance said. "I'd have to get up there and see how everything was going. I'd probably have to offer to join up with him. I'm a halfbreed, so he wouldn't find that hard to believe."

Crook sat down again. "You know I can't help you if anything happens. They don't love you in Washington, and that's a fact. You don't even have to go if you don't want to. It's getting to the point where there isn't much any man can do. The things men will do for money! I'd like to take certain parties I know and shoot them out of hand."

"I'd be there holding your coat, Three Stars. I don't know what I can do. It may be too big for any man. But I'd like to take a look. I could always kill Riel, but I'll face that when I come to it. How much do you really know about the man? I know what's in the newspapers, and that's all. You've obviously been studying up on him."

"As much as I can," the general said. "And I can't decide whether he's little crazy or big crazy. Some men are sane and crazy at the same time. Let me read you some of the notes I've made. You can't read my writing, so don't try."

"Louis Riel, born in 1844, son of Louis Riel and the daughter of the first white child born in the River Settlement. Said to be one-eighth Indian, though no proof exists of this. In 1858 sent to Sulpician College, in Montreal, to study for the priesthood. Moody, ill-tempered, wrote poetry. Left the seminary without completing his studies. On his way home to Red River worked as a clerk in a general store in St. Paul, Minnesota. Later became prominent in the *métis* (halfbreed) movement, its slogan was: 'For the first owners of the soil.' Began an association with Fenian leader W. B. O'Donoghue of Fort Garry. In 1870, now leader of the halfbreeds and Indians, Riel spoke of inviting annexation by the United States. After declaring a provisional government, Riel's forces were defeated and he was forced to flee Canada. After fifteen years in Montana, where he was a schoolteacher among other things, he recently returned to the North West Territories. During his exile, he spent two years in asylums and has been described as a religious fanatic with an often stated desire to establish his own church. Dark hair, wild staring black eyes, well educated, well spoken. Fluent in English and French. His whereabouts are not known at the present time."

General Crook put down the sheet of paper. "That's about it, Jim. He's more of a mystery than anything else. The Canadian government has tried to buy him off

21

with the finest tracts of land in the Territories, but he just laughs at them. They offered to settle a lifetime pension, a big one, on him if he will return to his country. Money means nothing to him. Riel always says, 'I will dress no better than the poorest of my people. I will eat what they eat, and if there is not enough for me I will eat nothing.' I'm not afraid of much, my old friend, but this man frightens me. Yes, kill him if you have to. How soon can you start?"

"Today."

"You'll need money."

"I have enough money to last me. If I take too much money, they may search me and find it. If I have to use the telegraph, where do I send the messages?"

"To the Western Union general office on State Street. Send them to Edward Bellson. The manager is the only one who knows who that is. He'll get them over here as fast as a horse can run. Your best way to get to Regina—Riel is said to be close to there—in by Canadian Pacific. I hope we aren't at war with England the next time we meet."

Crook walked outside with Sundance; the wind from the lake was still bone-rattling cold. "It's colder than this where you're going," the general said. "One more thing, Jim. If you can't do any good, then let it go. More than that I can't tell you. Sometimes, these things have to take their course, and there's nothing anybody can do. Cut your losses and come on back home. I'll be waiting to hear what you have to say. Let's hope it's good news."

The two men shook hands, and the sentry passed Sundance out through the gate. Sundance had the feeling that there was a long, hard, dangerous road ahead.

Three

Sundance stabled his horse and went to get something to eat. There was blinding sunshine, a sky without a cloud, and a wind that bit through the quilted wool coat he was wearing. The big Canadian Pacific locomotive clanged through the depot at Regina, a town so new that few of its buildings had been painted. In the air was the smell of raw wood and turpentine.

Men and animals thronged the main street, filling it from one side to the other. From the saloons came the tinny rattle of mechanical pianos. A man with a flowing beard was standing on a nail barrel, telling the passersby about God. Two drunken halfbreeds were fighting about something, and it took an enormous Mountie to get them to move on.

Sundance pushed his way into a saloon called the Cromarty Place, proprietor Angus McAdams, and fought his way to the bar. A long-necked Scotsman was serving up hot whiskies with sugar and lemon in them. He gave Sundance a cautious look.

"What'll yours be?"

"One of those," Sundance said, pointing at the steaming jug. "Not too much sugar."

Some of the men at the bar turned to look at Sundance. Most of the men in the saloon were white, and he could feel them measuring him with their eyes, inspecting his array of weapons. The bartender set down the hot whiskey in front of Sundance and named a price three times higher than it should have been. Sundance paid it without question.

He relaxed as the warmth of the whiskey flowed through him. It had been an easy trip from Chicago, but he wanted to stand around and have a drink before he did anything else. He was in a strange town, a town that was clearly edgy. It looked as if people were taking sides, deciding which way to run when the shooting started. Men eyed him as much as they eyed each other.

A drunk came in from the street and got a drink at the bar. To Sundance he looked like a halfbreed, but in this country there was no way to be sure about a man. A man who looked one thing often turned out to be another.

For such a small man, the drunk had a big mouth, and he wasn't bashful about using it. Some of the men edged away from him until there was a space on both sides. He got another whiskey and drank it, then looked along the bar to where Sundance was standing.

"Hello, my friend," he said in a heavy French-Canadian accent. "I ain't see you before, have I?"

Sundance said no and turned to look in the mirror behind the bar. On his first day in town he didn't want to be bothered by a drunk. There was something not right about this man. It was just a feeling, and it became stronger when the short man sidled down the bar until he was very close.

"It's all right, mister," he said. "I'm not trying to cadge drinks. I have enough money of my own."

"Glad to hear it," Sundance said.

The man lowered his voice. "You don't have to be

careful with me. You're a 'breed just like me. We're all in this together."

By now his voice was a whisper. "Are you here to join the movement?"

"What movement?"

"In these parts, there is only one, my friend. You are either with it or against it. It's all right, you can talk to me. I know the people you have come to see. I can take you to them." He gestured toward the whites at the bar. "Pretty soon it will be all over for them. No longer will they walk around as if they owned the world. Soon it will be all changed."

"Good! That's fine."

"What did you say?"

"I said everything's fine. It's also a nice day. I just want to drink my drink."

"But you don't understand what I'm talking about. Your friends are my friends. You are not from this country, so you will need help to find your friends. There is no need to give any names. Just nod yes that you have come to join the movement."

"I still don't know what you're talking about. Now I'd be obliged if you'd let me drink my drink. I won't ask you again."

For an instant, the man's bleary eyes were clear, then he smiled stupidly and said, "No offense, my friend. I was just trying to be friendly to a stranger. I don't care. I can drink someplace else."

He went out and Sundance finished his whiskey. Turning to go, he found himself confronted by a tough-faced farmer in a bright red coat. But it wasn't trouble after all. The farmer said in a Yankee accent, "Watch yourself with that feller, whoever you are. He's a police spy."

Four

"My name is Jacob Sawtelle," the man said, "and I hate to see any man taken in by the likes of him. I don't know why the Mounties hire such a man. Sometimes I think I'd have done a lot better to have stayed in Vermont. But you know how restless a man can get when the countryside starts filling up. I figured why not come out here to the Territories and enjoy some peace and quiet."

"You could always go back," Sundance said. "It's not that far."

"I'm here, and here I stay. The hardest thing is not taking sides. The *métis* are fine people but fierce tempered when they feel they've been wronged. It would be good to dive down in a storm cellar and wait for this to blow over. It won't. I can't see any hope of that. Well, I'd better get to the store and get on home. The missus is as nervous as a cat these days. Watch out for that spy. I hear he gets a cash bonus for every *métis* sympathizer he turns over to the police. He goes by the name of Val Lafleche, but I'd hardly say that was his real name."

The Vermont farmer went out. Sundance watched him all the way to a hardware store down the street. Lafleche was his idea of what a sneak looked like, which didn't mean that Sawtelle wasn't a police agent too. Probably, the whole region was crawling with spies and double-crossers, the way it had been on the Kansas-Missouri border just before the war. Officially, there was no war on yet, but from what General Crook had said, it was almost unavoidable. It was the same old story of government stupidity, and now many people were going to die because of it.

Getting to Riel wasn't going to be easy. Crook said the *métis* leader had his headquarters in a town called Batoche, far up the Red River, but he moved around to the other halfbreed settlements, never staying in one place for long, always traveling with a bodyguard of one-hundred heavily armed men. All were expert frontiersmen, all deadly shots after a lifetime of hunting with little ammunition in some of the hardest country in the world.

These were the men he had to face: bitter, resentful, suspicious of all strangers, for no stranger had ever given them an honest deal. Louis Riel was their hero, and they would kill without mercy to protect him. It was no use asking questions about Riel; if the Mounties didn't throw him in jail, some of the *métis* would probably put a knife in his back. What he had to do was ride out alone and go north along the Red River. That he was a halfbreed wouldn't help as much as General Crook thought it would. After all, he was no peace-loving *métis* trapper but a professional fighting man; the *métis* would recognize that the moment they saw him.

Riel would probably know who he was, that is, if he lived long enough to be brought to the rebel headquarters. It wasn't likely any of the others would. Most were trappers and farmers; few spoke English. Sundance's plan, such as it was, was to offer his services to the *métis*. If they were working with the Fenians, they might have no hesitation in accepting him. He would just have to try it out.

He was strolling around town when something made him turn. He saw the man called Val Lafleche ducking behind a freight wagon. The movement was fast but awkward, as if Lafleche wanted to be seen. Lafleche had done nothing to attract Sundance's attention. Maybe he knew that a man like Sundance would know he was being followed. Sights and sounds had nothing to do with it. It was mostly instinct.

Sundance went into a small, crowded restaurant and sat at one of the six stools at the counter after a man picking his teeth got up and went out. After a long wait, the counter girl brought him a thick steak with hashed potatoes and coffee. In the steamed-up mirror behind the counter, he spotted Lafleche looking in the window. Then he ducked away as he had before. There was no doubt about it now. The sneak couldn't have been easier to see if he'd been beating a bass drum and foaming at the mouth.

Sundance waited for Lafleche to show his ugly face again, but he didn't. Then another man came in, as Sundance knew he would. There was nothing about him to attract attention. He was neither tall nor short, had sandy hair and a face like a thousand others, about forty years of age. He sat at a table against the wall and ordered coffee and a sandwich.

This was the real police spy, Sundance knew. How many there were in Regina he had no way of knowing. There might even be another to back this one up, but he didn't think so. The nondescript man looked as if he could handle it all by himself.

Sundance wondered if the Mounties already had some information about him. Or it could be that they simply watched every stranger who came to Regina, especially if he happened to be a heavily armed halfbreed from below the border? They said the Mounties were the best police in the world. Sundance had never thought about it. He knew he didn't want to tangle with them if he didn't have to, but he couldn't get anything done if he let them walk in his footsteps.

He paid for his meal and walked out as if going nowhere in particular. The police spy followed him outside and walked along behind him, varying the distance now and then. Sundance didn't try any fancy stopping and starting. He simply walked and let the police agent follow him. He didn't think the man would give up, even if they walked around all day, which was the last thing Sundance had in mind.

Sundance went into the Menteith Hotel and paid double for a small, clean room with a tinted picture of Queen Victoria on the wall. A few weak gasps of hot air came from a grating in the floor. The bed was narrow and hard; Sundance stretched out on it and waited for it to get dark.

Four hours later, the darkness of the northern winter came down rapidly, blurring the raw outlines of the town. He went to the door and listened for sounds in the hall. A door banged and somebody went downstairs in heavy boots. On the first floor, plates and silverware clattered as the waitresses prepared for the evening meal.

The back of the hotel faced a patch of woods where snow was packed hard between the trees. Sundance pushed up the window and looked out. If they were waiting, there was no sign of them. Nothing moved but pine branches and snow crystals stirred by the wind. It seemed to have gotten warmer; that could mean more snow. They could track him a lot easier in snow, Sundance realized; but they could track him anyway if they had the right man—and they would.

Buckling on his weapons belt over his thick woolen coat, Sundance pulled on his gloves, figured the drop, and let go the windowsill. He landed lightly in packed snow and ran quickly to the cover of a stack of lumber. No one yelled at him to stop.

He went along behind the hotel, across the mouth of an alley, and kept going until he was in back of the livery stable. An alley ran between the stable and a freight office next door. He went into the alley but stopped before he got to the street. Down the street, on the far side, was the stone bulk of the North West Mounted Police barracks with two Gatling guns drawn up in front of it. There was the crash of heavy boots as the police sentries changed guard.

From the alley, Sundance watched the far side of the street. A lumber yard with a fence around it stood dark and quiet, locked up for the night. No lights showed anywhere in the two-story buildings, and the gate was closed. He backed away quickly when he heard the faint noise of a horse pawing the ground. If the wind had been blowing the other way, he wouldn't have heard it at all.

There it was. They were in there waiting for him to get his horse and come out the front door of the stable. Then they would ride after him. Sundance smiled and hoped they wouldn't get too cold waiting there in the dark and thinking of hot food and the heavily sugared tea Canadians liked so much.

Back behind the stable, he inspected the padlock on the door. It was sturdy and the wood was new, but he figured his hatchet blade would pry it loose. It had to be done quietly, or the livery man would start shooting or yelling for the Mounties. One was as bad as the other.

He put his ear to the door and listened for sounds inside. At first there was nothing, then he heard the sound of snoring. The snoring went on interspersed with a loud snort every so often. This was the best chance he would get, Sundance knew, because it was always possible that the police would decide to look in his room. If they found him, they could toss him in jail until the trouble with Riel was over. That could be months. If it came to a showdown, he knew he wouldn't kill any Mounties.

Working carefully but steadily, he dug his keen-bladed hatchet into the door, stopping occasionally to listen for sounds. Wind hummed in telegraph wires at the front of the stable. Nothing else was heard. He was sweating in spite of the cold when the hasp of the lock began to come free of the wood. It moved some more when he slid the blade of the hatchet under the hasp and used the handle as a lever. Another short pull on the handle was all it took to open the door.

The stable had horse stalls on both sides of a central open area. In a corner a man lay on a cot under a huge pile of blankets, a whiskey bottle on the floor beside him. There was no heat of any kind, and the only light came from a lantern turned down low. The front door was barred from the inside.

Sundance squinted through the crack between the two halves of the door. Across the street, the lumber yard was dark, its gate still closed. Powdered snow blew in the wagon ruts in the hard-frozen mud.

Sundance spoke quitely to the other horses in the stable, soothing the animals while he saddled Eagle. On the cot the stable man muttered in his sleep. Sundance stayed perfectly still in Eagle's stall while the man, with his eyes closed, reached down for the whiskey bottle and took a long drink. "Damn, it's cold," he grumbled.

In moments, he was snoring again.

Sundance closed the back door of the stable and put a board against it to keep it closed. It wouldn't be long before they traced him from the hotel to the stable. Their big advantage was that they knew the country and he didn't, not at all.

There was only one way to get out, and that was to do it head-on. Once he got out of town, he would have to look for Mountie patrols and head for the Red River. From the maps he had looked at, the Red River would take him north to Batoche. If he didn't find Riel there, he would have to keep on looking, that is, if some *métis* sharpshooter didn't knock him out of the saddle at a long distance.

It was rough country up on the Red River: during the winter it was frozen solid for five months. To be caught out there unprepared or injured was to die. The Red River was a land without mercy for the stranger.

Sundance had some supplies but he hadn't loaded up too heavily because that would have attracted suspicion. Few men were going north in the Territories with war about to break out. What he hoped for was to buy food at *métis* farmhouses along the way or to shoot what small game he could find.

Leading Eagle, he went into the woods behind the town and kept going until there were no longer any lights or sounds. Then he found the road and mounted up, heading northwest toward the river. Finding the Red River would be easy. After that, he'd be facing a frozen hell.

Five

An Arctic wind swept into the town of Batoche, sending flurries of snow down the chimney of Louis Riel's thick-walled log cabin. Riel sat by the fire talking to the New York Irishman, Colum Hardesty, who had come so far to strike a blow at the hated English.

Hardesty was in his late thirties, big bones, black haired and blue eyed. Even in a chair, he moved with a sort of swagger. His voice was deep and musical. When he made a point, he had the habit of punching his right fist into the palm of the left.

A big iron pot of stew was bubbling, suspended over the fire by a crane. Outside, the wind strained against the door and rattled the shutters. The two oil lamps flickered as the wind grew stronger.

Hardesty ladled stew into a bowl and cut a chunk of bread from a loaf. "I'm telling you it can be done, Louis," he said. "All through history, men have been doing things other men said couldn't be done. Now is the time to free your people once and for all, but you must act decisively. Show the Canadians that you won't stand for any more of their false promises."

Riel smiled, "I think you are more concerned with the

British than the Canadians. You know this, but I will tell you anyway. Our quarrel is with the Canadians and not the British. As long as the British controlled the North West Territories, they treated us fairly. It was when they handed the Territories over to the Canadians that our troubles began. The British are harsh but fair, while the Canadians are too much like the Americans—and much less honest."

"Action is what your people need, not words," Hardesty said impatiently. "What does it matter who rules you if you're not free to rule yourselves? This can be a time of greatness for you, a chance to create a government of your own without interference from Ottawa or London."

"What about Washington and this talk of annexation? You say you have guarantees from certain people in America. And why would the Americans be any better than the Canadians? The Canadians never treated the Indians as badly as the Americans."

Hardesty said, "The independence of the North West Territories has been guaranteed. This is in appreciation for your help. Annexation is going to take place anyway. It's always been inevitable, so now is the time to strike a blow for freedom."

"For Ireland? Ireland is so far away. I am afraid your country doesn't mean much to me. If it comes to that, many of the Canadians are Irish. The Irish are Catholics, as we are, but they have taken sides against us. I must be honest with you, Colum, I must tell you that my only concern is for the *métis*, my own people. We fight our own fights and always have."

"And you should be honored for it," Hardesty said, "but this isn't fifteen years ago, when you first tried to shake off the Canadians. Now Canada has grown powerful. What you are facing is no longer a series of skirmishes but battles. And guerrilla warfare isn't the answer. You know yourself the country here is too harsh. In British Columbia it would be different. No, Louis, if you are going to fight the Canadians and win against them, you are going to need all the help you can get. That means men and money."

"And annexation?"

"Call it intervention. The United States is a nation of businessmen. What you must do is exchange economic benefits for military and political pressure. *You* will get independence for the North West Territories, and the Americans will make money."

Riel said, "They broke every treaty they made with the Indians. According to the U.S. Constitution, every state had the right to secede. But look what happened to the South when it tried: crushed, ruined, degraded."

Hardesty said, "You have a point. But I don't see how you can win any other way. Anyway, the North West Territories aren't the South. The real reason the North attacked the South was to seize control of its agriculture and its trade. The Americans would scarcely fight that hard to take your Territories. Marching through Georgia isn't like marching up the Red River with the temperature at twenty below."

Riel smiled at the Irishman. "Yes, we have that in our favor. Yet, if men want something badly enough, they will do almost anything."

Hardesty smacked one hand into the other. "That's what I've been telling you. You've made your own point, now let me make another, which is that this is probably the last chance you'll ever get to free your people. Already, the Canadian Pacific has come through. But railroad tracks can be dynamited, bridges blown up, tunnels caved in. That can all be done to prevent the Canadian troop movements that are sure to come. But I'm not just talking about railroads, I'm talking about tens of thousands of people moving into the Territories.

35

They'll bury your people with their numbers."

Riel stared into the fire as though looking for answers. "You're right, of course," he said. "They will bury us if we—I—let them. I don't want you to be right about some of the things you've said, but you are. But this last thing I must think about. A general Indian uprising could be a terrible thing, more terrible than the war we are planning against the Canadians, much more savage."

Hardesty was stubborn, hard eyed. "It's all part of the same war. The Sioux, the Blackfoot, the Cree, and the Assiniboin all want to strike at the whites."

"All I want is a measure of freedom for my people," Riel said. "There was a time when I would have accepted limited independence. It was never my intention to rebel against the authority of the central government, but they forced me. If only they would let us go, withdraw their mounted police, take their steamboats from our rivers, and leave us in peace."

"You're dreaming when you talk like that," Hardesty said. "In Ireland, all we asked was the same thing. We had our own parliament, were loyal to the king, and then they dissolved it because a few greedy men wanted it that way. Now, eighty-five years later, my country is in poverty."

Louis Riel spooned some stew into a dish and proceeded to eat it without much enthusiasm. "We have talked enough for the moment about ideas and old wrongs. It is time to be practical. These Fenians of yours, will they fight? I know they have the will to fight, but what if they have to fight Canadian regulars?"

Riel's voice was apologetic. "Your Fenians tried to take Canada nearly twenty years ago. When was it? 1867. They were defeated and driven back across the border. 'General' O'Neill did not lead his men very well."

Anger glinted in Hardesty's eyes. "O'Neill was a fool and certainly no general. The men he lead on this comic-opera invasion were mostly hooligans from the slums of New York. Some had served in the Union Army in volunteer regiments. The men I have coming here are all ex-regulars, many of them veterans of the Indian Wars. They are all well trained and will be well paid. Some are Fenians, some are not. I don't care what they are as long as they fight. I will lead them under your command, and we will win. I didn't spend seven years in the British army just for nothing. I joined because I wanted to learn how to fight. There was no chance to become an officer, but I read every book I could find on tactics and military history. I've been preparing for this day a very long time."

Riel said, "It is not good to have so much hate, Colum. You have to learn to fight the enemy without hating him. That makes you better than he is."

Hardesty laughed. "You fight your way, Louis, and I'll fight mine. What would be the good of fighting your enemy if you didn't hate him? After Ireland wins her independence, I'll write a letter to the Queen and tell her what a fine, fat old lady she is. But until then..."

"How will the men get here?" Riel asked.

"Obviously, not all together and not from the same direction. Some will go north from Boston to Montreal and Ottawa and from there all the way west by Canadian Pacific. Others will come in through Minnesota and Montana. I have men from San Francisco who will go north to Vancouver and take the railroad over the mountains from there. None are halfbreeds, so they shouldn't attract much attention."

"And the guns?"

"The guns will be here. Modern military rifles, Gatling guns. Maxim guns if I can get them, but I hardly think so. There are Maxims in some of the eastern arsenals. I will have word from Ottawa. A friend of the movement—yours and mine—is a sergeant of supply. If we had Maxims, we could really turn this war against them."

"You haven't mentioned artillery. The militia is well equipped with artillery. I don't see how we can stand up against it."

Hardesty didn't look so confident. "The only way we can get artillery is to capture it. Rapid-fire guns can be dismantled and moved easily enough. Artillery is too heavy. What we have to aim for is speed and surprise. Do what they don't expect. Don't dig into fortifications unless there is no other way. We have to gain control of the forts and mounted-police barracks. That's where their strength is—and their weakness, too. If we can pin them down, they will run out of food and will be forced to surrender. Your people can last a lot longer without food than they can."

"There must be no massacre, Colum. I don't care what happens. I won't tolerate that, even if we have to lose the war."

"It will be hard to take prisoners, Louis. Where would we keep them? If we turn them loose, especially the Mounties, they will be back breathing fire. My motto is: Show a man mercy and he'll kill you for it. Besides, if we kill them, there will be no way back, not for you, not for me, not for any of us."

"And if we lose?"

"They will hang us by the dozen, send hundreds to prison for the rest of their lives. So there's no way out, even if we don't kill the prisoners. It may sound brutal, but in the end it's very practical. When a man has a chance to surrender, he may or may not take it. When he hasn't, there is nothing to be lost but his life, so he fights on."

"Until he's dead. Until we're all dead? Is that what you're saying without really saying it, Colum? Do you want to die in a blaze of glory. You may not know that's really what you want."

"Now you're talking wild, Louis. That's the last thing I want. What I want is a nice soft job in your administration when you take over. How does that sound?"

Riel said, "That's the last thing you want. You want that no more than I do."

"You're right, Louis. That's not what I want."

"You can't kill the prisoners," Louis Riel said firmly. "If that's what you want to do, then we must part company. There will be enough killing as it is. That is my decision, only one of the many I have to make. Another thing I must tell you so you can tell it to your friends in Washington. If we defeat the Canadians and the Americans follow them, then we will fight them too. That must be understood."

Hardesty looked sullen, at the point of insubordination. "Since you're getting things in order, we'd better talk about Gabriel Dumont."

"Talk about what? You have alread raised the question of Dumont, and I gave my answer. I though it was settled."

"But he isn't qualified to command your army."

"And you are?"

"I'm better qualified than he is."

"Yes, I know you served in the British Army for seven years, in Africa and India. That's not the point. Gabriel Dumont has been part of this movement for more than fifteen years. He's a fighter, and he knows men, especially the *métis*. In a way, fighting and the *métis* are all he knows. He will be a good commander, believe me."

"I wish I could, Louis. I don't mean that disrespectfully, but you are not a soldier."

"Colum," Riel said, "if Gabriel or I don't lead the *métis* in battle, they won't fight. I could lead them, but what good would that do? It has to be Gabriel Dumont."

"My men may not want to serve under him?"

"Why? Because he's a halfbreed?"

"They would rather serve under me. Some of them have known me for a long time; at least the ones from New

York and Boston have. What do you think of the idea?"

"I will have to think about it. Now let me tell you something, and this must be said so there won't be any misunderstandings. You will not play politics with my people. I am not saying that is your intention, but men have a way of changing when the stakes get big enough. If I say Gabriel Dumont commands, that decision is final. Another thing, and I regret to say it, if you want to back out of this, now is the time. There is no ill will in anything I say."

"I didn't think there was, Louis. We were just talking, clearing the air, as they say."

A fist banged on the door and Hardesty jumped up with a Colt .45 in his hand. He motioned Riel away from the line of fire, if it came.

"It's Gabriel Dumont," a rough voice called out. "I think we have a spy. Open the door."

Hardesty unbarred the door and Jim Sundance, half numb with cold, was shoved inside.

Looking at his yellow hair and copper skin, Hardesty said, "Well now, what have we here?"

Six

"Look at the weapons he was carrying," Gabriel Dumont said, putting the Colt .44, throwing hatchet, and Bowie knife on the table. "He has a .44 Winchester and an Indian bow. They're with his horse, a fine stallion. He tried to kill me when I got close to him."

Hardesty, sizing up Sundance, asked, "Where did you find him?"

Dumont said, "Half frozen in the stable of the old Heber farm—down by the river. We were half frozen too. The snow was beginning to let up by then. No, he didn't try to resist. It wouldn't have done any good if he had. He'd better have some food and coffee. Is there any stew left?"

"Enough," Hardesty answered.

"You'd better sit down," he told Sundance, handing him a cup of black coffee. "Now, my lad, you'd better come up with some believable answers, or you'll never see daylight. Who are you and what do you want? Our friend here thinks you're a spy. I think so, too. First, your name?"

"Jim Sundance?"

"From where?"

"All over. I know all over is a big place, but it's true."

"We'll see about that." Hardesty jerked a thumb at Riel. "Naturally, you wouldn't know who this gentleman is?"

"Louis Riel. I know who he is."

"I'll bet you do. And you came all this way to join up with him?"

"I had that idea. Everybody knows what he's trying to do. I belong here more than you do. You're not a halfbreed."

Hardesty smiled. "I'm a green halfbreed. Now, Mr. James Sundance, how did you get all the way up here? You didn't come through Regina."

"That's how I came."

"And the Mounties didn't stop you, a halfbreed armed to the teeth?"

Sundance said, "A police spy followed me around after I arrived in town. I managed to get away from him."

"How?"

After Sundance explained, Hardesty said, "You're tricky all right, too tricky even for the Mounties. My opinion is that you're too tricky to live."

"Did you see anybody else?" Hardesty asked Gabriel Dumont.

It was obvious to Sundance that there was bad blood between the Irishman and the halfbreed. "You are asking plenty of questions, Hardesty. While I was catching this prisoner or spy—I don't know—you were sitting by the fire. But I will answer your question. There was nobody with him. If there had been, my men would have been back by now."

"Next time you can sit by the fire," said Hardesty. "You captured this man. Do you think he's a spy—for the Mounties or the militia? I think he is, but you don't have to agree with me."

"You don't have to tell me that. Yes, I think he's a spy. There is no reason to think he is not. He is not one of our people, and no other American halfbreeds have offered to fight for us. I think he was sent here to do harm to our cause, perhaps to kill our leader. There is only one way to deal with spies." Gabriel Dumont shrugged. "And if it turns out that he is not a spy, what difference will it make?"

"My own sentiments," Hardesty said. "But I'd like to ask our visitor a few more questions."

"Ask away," Sundance said. "You won't believe me anyway."

Hardesty continued. "It doesn't make sense for you to come up here and try to walk in without a name to recommend you. Give us a name, some name that we know. It would be dumb for a man to come up here without a name to pass him through. What about it? Was it Fournier in Fort Garry? McBride in Toronto?"

Sundance said he didn't know the names.

Hardesty said, "And it's no wonder, since there are no such people. "It isn't looking too hopeful for you, Mr. James Sundance. A fanciful name that. Did you make it up yourself?"

"What did you see in Regina?" Hardesty asked. "You'll probably tell us you saw five regiments of militia. Be honest now, tell us what you saw."

Sundance said, "No militia, just mounted police. There are two Gatling guns in front of the barracks."

Hardesty glanced over at Louis Riel, who hadn't said anything. "Well, I suppose you did pass through Regina after all. We know about the two Gatlings. Knew since they were brought there on the train. We know about the militia, too."

Gabriel Dumont was becoming impatient, but he ate his stew in silence. Riel was staring at Sundance with a puzzled look on his face.

Hardesty started again. "You have blond hair. How did you get that?"

43

"My father had yellow hair. I got it from him."

"Frenchmen aren't usually blond."

"My father was English."

"So you're half English, are you. That means I hate you only half as much as a regular Englishman."

Turning to Gabriel Dumont, the Irishman said, "That was a joke."

Hardesty asked, "And what's the other half of you?"

"Cheyenne," Sundance answered.

Dumont said slowly, "You are a long way from your mother's people. It would have been better if you had stayed there."

"I'm beginning to believe that."

"It's a bit late for that," Hardesty said. "We can't let you stay, and we can't let you ride out. So you know what it has to be. We're going to have to kill you. But first there will be more questions. I think you're a goddamned liar. But before you go, you're going to tell the truth. You're going to tell us who really sent you and how many more men there are like you. You're going to tell us about the things you've seen. By the time we get through with you, you'll be begging for death."

Gabriel Dumont put down his fork and took out a skinning knife from a slender sheath. He held it over the chimney of a lamp until it began to glow white hot.

"Wait a minute," Hardesty said, "we'll try the easy, the humane way first. A man talks more sensibly if he isn't in agony. But you will be in a minute if you don't talk. Keep the knife hot, Gabriel."

Hardesty stood over Sundance, "Now, my friend, the name of the man who sent you. Mountie or militia, it doesn't matter. I want his name, because we're going to send a man to kill him. I want his name and the men who work under him. It's time they learned that they can't just send spies in here pretending to be patriots. What's his name?"

"There is no man."

"What's his name? His name and all the others?"

"I can't tell you. There's nothing to tell."

Hardesty pointed to Dumont's thin-bladed knife. "We're just wasting our time. Go to work on Mr. James Sundance, and see how he likes it."

Sundance started to sweat as the glowing blade came close to his face. He could already feel its white hot edge.

"Wait!" Louis Riel shouted, standing up. "I think I know this man."

Seven

Riel came over to where Sundance was standing and said, "You say your name is James Sundance."

"Jim Sundance. People call me Sundance."

"And you are of the Cheyenne?"

"My mother was."

Gabriel Dumont was still holding the knife. Riel waved it away.

"You know this man, Louis?" Hardesty said, looking doubtful.

"Perhaps," Riel said. "When I first heard the name, it meant nothing to me. Now I am not so sure."

To Sundance he said, "Your name has been in the newspapers in the United States. When I was in Montana I heard your name, something about your fight against the Indian Ring in Washington. Are you the same Jim Sundance?"

Sundance said he was.

"Anybody can use a name," Hardesty said. "You have used many names yourself, Louis. So have I. So has Gabriel."

"Never," Gabriel Dumont growled, waving the knife in the air to let it cool. "My name is my own."

Outside, the wind whipped against the walls of the cabin as if it were trying to kill those inside. Powdered snow sifted in under the bottom of the door. It was quiet except for the wind and the crackling of the fire.

Riel raised his hand in a command for silence, his forehead creased in thought. "What was your father's name?" he asked Sundance.

"Nicholas."

Riel said, "Many years ago, when I was a boy on the Red River, I knew a man of that name. My father had a mill and a man of that name, an Englishman, worked for him. He had a Cheyenne wife and there was a son. Are you that son?"

"I don't know," Sundance said. "If I was, I don't remember. My father worked at many things, at many trades. We were in many places. I know we were in Canada at one time. I think I was about five at that time."

"I am forty," Riel said, "and that would be about right. I was about ten then, and I remember an Englishman, an Indian woman, and a child with yellow hair. I don't know how long they stayed. It was not long. There was a scar on the man's hand. I can't remember which hand."

"A long scar on the palm of the left hand," Sundance said. "A drunken buffalo hunter tried to stab my father, and he blocked the thrust with his hand. He told me about the scar when I asked him. His hand gave him pain all his life."

"You could be who you say you are," Riel said, staring at Sundance as if by doing so he could relive the events of thirty years before. The *métis* leader's face was clouded in thought.

Hardesty cut in with, "A scar on a man's hand! What does that prove? It proves nothing to me. It could all be a plan to hoodwink you. Ask him something else."

"Please, Colum," Riel said mildly, still looking at Sundance with his bright black eyes. "What book did

47

your father always carry in his pocket, the one he read while he was eating?"

"The Bible," Sundance answered. "My father was not a religious man, Mr. Riel, but the Bible was his favorite book. In it, he always said, was enough reading for a man's lifetime. There was enough even if a man lived to be a very old man."

"And the color of the cover? Was it black?"

"No. Dark red."

"Do you want some coffee, Sundance?" Riel asked, turning to get the pot.

"Listen, Louis," Hardesty said. "If the Mounties or the militia sent this man, they would tell him things like that: the scar on the hand, the Bible.

Riel handed a cup to Sundance. "Things that happened thirty years ago? A Bible with a red cover? I hardly think so, my untrusting friend."

The Irishman protested: "All right, maybe he is who he says he is. I'll grant you the scar and the Bible. Does all that prove that he isn't a spy or an assassin? A hired killer sent by the Canadians to murder you? Back in Ireland, I knew of a man who took money to kill his own brothers, two of our organization. He killed one, but we got him before he killed the other. Louis, you're not risking just your own life. You're putting the whole movement in danger. I say kill him now."

Riel said, "You're so ready to kill, my friend. I will remind you that I have not survived fifteen years with a price on my head by being a fool."

"I still say I'm right."

Riel's voice was still unemotional. "If you are right, then we will kill him. Is he right, Sundance?"

"No."

"Do you believe him, Gabriel?"

Dumont said, "I don't know. I trust you, Louis. You are our leader. Say kill him and it will be done."

"That's mighty obliging of you," Hardesty said to Dumont.

"I wasn't talking to you, Irishman."

Riel said, "The war isn't in here, gentleman, and name calling won't help us win it."

Hardesty said, "We don't need this man to win it."

For the first time Riel's dark eyes displayed anger. "We're going to need all the men we can get, and if this man is Jim Sundance, he's worth ten of your paid soldiers. Wars are not won with money but with the heart. Sometimes I think you forget that Colum. For you, I think, war is more important than the winning of it. I have been called many things in my lifetime, but I do not love war. If the Canadians would let us go, there would be no killing. To wage war is what you have to do when all else fails."

Looking at Riel, listening to his formal way of talking, Sundance thought of what Crook had said about the *métis* leader. He had spent nearly two years in an asylum, wanted to start his own church, talked about his divine mission. He was ready to take on a powerful government with a few hundred halfbreeds. A white man might have decided that Riel was mad, but Sundance wasn't so sure. After his own parents had been tortured and killed by renegades, he himself had been close to crazy for a while, drinking heavily, courting death at every opportunity. If George Crook hadn't knocked the craziness out of his dead, he would almost certainly be dead by now. Grief often drove a man crazy. It was clear that Louis Riel was tormented by what had happened to his people—robbed of their land, degraded by the whiskey traders from the States, left without hope.

"You served as a scout for the army?" Riel said to Sundance, pouring more coffee. "As a scout and a hunter?"

"With General Crook, in many campaigns."

"Then you fought against your own people?" Hardesty cut in angrily. "Now you want to fight *for* them, is that it? What made you change your mind, turncoat? Was it because you thought there was money to be made by working for both sides?"

Sundance said, "I have fought for and against the Indians. With Crook it was different. I worked for the General because that was the only way I could help my people."

Hardesty said, "Crook killed plenty of Indians while he was talking out of both sides of his mouth. At least Sheridan was honest when he said he'd like to see them all dead. Now I'll be honest with you, friend. I'd like to see you dead."

Riel lay back in his chair and ran thin fingers through his hair. Lines of worry and sadness furrowed his cheeks; his eyes were very tired. His dark clothes were stained with mud; only his moccasins looked fit for this hard northern country.

"You're wrong about General Crook. When he gave his word, he kept it. Do you know that he once hanged four whiskey traders in the Dakotas for selling poisoned whiskey to the Sioux? Many Indians went blind or died in agony. Crook didn't waste any time. He led the four white men to a tree and they were hanged. The incident almost cost him his career. Do you remember that, Sundance?"

"I was with him when it happened. It was where the town of Deadwood is now. The whiskey traders worked for the Indian Ring in Washington. When they heard about it, they tried everything they could to get him cashiered, but Sheridan backed him up."

"How do you balance four dead whites against I don't know how many thousands of dead Indians?" Hardesty said. "Did Crook do it because his heart was so pure? Or was it because he hated the Indian Ring for political reasons? Nothing is ever what it seems to be, Louis. What does it matter what this man did in the past? We're talking about the here and now, which is all that matters. It's your decision to make, but I'll say it again. Get rid of him. He smells of death."

Riel said calmly, "He certainly looks like a dangerous man. Are you, Sundance?"

"So I've been told. What's it going to be? Do I stay or get a bullet in the back?"

"There will be no bullets in the back. If you give us cause to kill you, then you will be judged and executed by a firing squad. You will have a chance to face your executioners. You want an answer and I can't give you one. Not yet."

Gesturing toward Hardesty and Dumont, Riel said, "These men are my friends, and I must consider what they have said. For the moment you can stay, but you will be watched all the time."

Hardesty grunted with sour satisfaction. "That's better. He'll be watched all right, and I'll do most of the watching."

Dumont nodded silently as he put the thin-bladed skinning knife back in its sheath. Sundance knew he hadn't made an enemy in the scowling halfbreed; Dumont was just a hard-eyed man who would kill him for the good of the cause, if it came to that. Hardesty was different. Sundance thought he knew why the scheming Irishman wanted to kill him. Hardesty figured that somehow he would get between him and Riel. Probably the Irishman figured Dumont could be pushed aside or, failing that, killed and buried in some lonely place. Riel could then be made into a puppet. If he failed to jump when Hardesty pulled the strings, another more easily managed *métis* leader could be found. Here in the North West Territories, there was great wealth; the man who controlled it could live like a king. That would be, Sundance decided, the Irishman's way of thinking, since

51

there was always a faint undercurrent of contempt when he spoke to Riel.

"Do I get to keep my weapons?" Sundance asked Riel, nodding toward the pistol, knife, and hatchet on the table.

"You won't need them for the moment," Riel answered. "If I decide you can stay, you'll get them back. Nothing will be stolen from you here. There will be food and a warm place to sleep. Do not attempt to leave the camp at any time, even to walk over to the village. The sentries will shoot if you do. Their orders are firm. Other than that, you may move freely about the camp"—Riel smiled—"since nothing you see can ever be reported. Now Gabriel will show you where you are to be billeted. I will talk to you again tomorrow."

The snow had stopped by the time Sundance and Dumont left the cabin. Hardesty stayed behind to talk to Riel. Stars were beginning to appear in the deep-black sky; the wind whipped through the pines, knifing through their clothes. Now it was possible to see what the camp looked like. Except that the buildings were all made of rough-hewn logs, it didn't look much different from an army encampment. There were barracks on three sides and a wide space in the center. Several hundred yards away was the beginning of the village of Batoche. It was late, and no lights showed in the windows. A frozen river gleamed in the moonlight; the snow under their feet already had a crust on it. In the village, a dog barked furiously and then was joined by another dog. They both stopped. The only sound was the wind howling down from the Arctic wastes.

"Look where you're going," Dumont yelled above the sound of the wind. "Those are trenches."

Sundance looked and saw the outlines of long rows of trenches, now completely filled with snow. In the barracks on the north side, only one light was burning.

Sundance was still chilled, even after the food and coffee. The thought of rolling up in thick blankets looked better every time he braced himself against a fresh blast of wind.

"Your horse is all right," Dumont said, plodding through deep snow with the patience of a man who has lived with it all his life. "Warm, well looked after—a fine animal."

Nothing else was said until they were close to the barracks. "You will sleep in my cabin," Dumont said. "There is another bunk. You would like something else to eat? There was not much stew."

"I could use it," Sundance said. "Anything—not necessarily something hot."

"You would eat a bear steak raw?"

"Not unless I had to. I've seen it done."

Leading the way to his quarters, Dumont said, "That was a Gatling gun you were looking at back there. Soon we will have others."

Sundance had seen the rapid-fire gun, a hump in the snow wrapped in blankets and covered with tarpaulin covers. He had wondered why nobody was guarding it. A rapid-fire gun was worth an additional thirty men. Then he knew the reason it wasn't guarded. Batoche was two-hundred miles north of Regina; no force of Mounties would travel more than a few miles without being spotted by unseen lookouts.

"We will soon have more Gatling guns and many more men," Dumont said, opening the door of the warm cabin. He banged the door against the wind and barred it, then placed a stack of logs on the fire. The seasoned wood took hold immediately, sending sparks flying up the massive stone chimney. Dumont turned up the wick of the lamp, revealing a long, cluttered, low-ceilinged room. Rifles and bayonets, even sabers and daggers, hung from pegs driven into the walls. A skinny dog stretched lazily in front of the fire. There was a smell of sweat and cooking. In this cabin there were no books; Riel's cabin had been littered with them.

"That is my bunk," Dumont said, pointing to a roughly built platform covered with a buffalo robe. "Yours is there. Put on more blankets if you are cold. But it won't be cold. The *métis* know how to keep out the cold. Do you want a drink of whiskey?"

Sundance said yes.

"I would like to drink whiskey, but I dare not," Dumont said. "Now that I am a leader, I dare not. Whiskey does something to my head. At first for a while I am happy, then a rage takes possession of me. So I dare not drink. But when this war is over, I am going to go far north to a cabin I once built, and there I will be drunk for a month or until the whiskey is gone. Up there I will bother no one, hurt no one, except the bears."

Sundance decided that Dumont looked more like a bear than a man. He was built like a grizzly, was barrel chested, and had a big shaggy head set squarely on a short, thick neck—obviously a man of tremendous strength. A brute, but an intelligent brute.

While two big bear steaks were frying in skillets, Dumont gathered all the weapons from the walls and locked them in a long box that looked like a coffin. "So you will not be tempted," he said, turning the steaks and adding seasoning.

He pointed. "The whiskey and glasses are in the cupboard. Drink as much as you like, but please do not make sounds of enjoyment. It would sadden me if you did."

Sundance got the whiskey and a glass. He uncorked the bottle. The whiskey had a strong smell and no color: moonshine. He poured a glass and drank it carefully. It was easy not to make sounds of enjoyment. What wasn't easy was to get it down.

54

Dumont speared the bear steaks and served them up smoking hot. The look and smell of the properly seasoned meat made Sundance forget the foul taste of the whiskey, because when bear meat is aged and cooked just right, there is nothing else as good. This steak was tender enought for Sundance to cut it with the side of his fork.

They ate in silence for a while. Now and then, Dumont wiped his mouth with the back of his hand. When he finished, he threw scraps of meat to the dog, then put the plates in a tin basin of soapy water. Later he climbed into his bunk after lighting a long clay pipe. Sundance was already covered up by five blankets, a great weariness creeping over him. It had been one hell of a trip from Regina.

Dumont asked, "Was the whiskey to your liking? And the steak?"

"Everything was fine," Sundance answered, opening his eyes to look at the other man. There was neither friendship nor hostility in the halfbreed's eyes. He just wanted to be sure Sundance had enjoyed his meal.

Maybe my last meal, Sundance thought sleepily. In the morning, Dumont might have to kill him.

Eight

Dumont was brewing strong tea when Sundance woke up in the morning. It was the smell of the tea that woke him more than anything else. The halfbreed had made two pots, one for Sundance, one for himself. The fire had been built up again, and the cabin was warm; the windows were clear of snow.

Sundance pulled on his shirt and pants and watched impassively while Dumont cut slices of black-plug tobacco and dropped them into the already boiled-black tea. He had heard of this custom, which was said to exist among the hermit trappers of the North West and Alaska, but he had always thought it was just another tall tale from remote places.

Sundance's own black tea was ready to drink; he didn't add sugar or milk, as was the custom in the north. He didn't much like any kind of tea, but it was a cold morning and the tea was hot.

"You have never tried this?" Dumont said, putting the metal pot back on the bed of coals at the front of the fire. Immediately, it began to bubble, and the smell was no longer that of tea.

"No," Sundance said, adding that he wasn't ready to try.

56

"You have to get used to it," Dumont explained, stirring the awful-looking mixture, "and you must have a strong heart. I have known of men with weak hearts who were killed by it." The big halfbreed thumped his barrel-shaped chest. "I have a heart like a bull buffalo. It gives me great energy, but my heart remains steady. Once, when I was badly injured in the woods and couldn't hunt, I lived on it for ten days. In all that time, I never felt hunger. If you drink enough of it, you can go without sleep for days."

Dumont paused. "It can also make a man crazy. One time in the Yukon, I came across an old hunter running naked in the snow. It was a bitter cold day with a strong wind. I grabbed him and dragged him back to his cabin before he froze to death. Beside the fire was a whole bucket of this tea. There was snuff in it, too. I had to tie him to his bunk to keep him from running out again. He kept saying his body was on fire, and the only way to cool off was to run in the snow. It took him two days before he was able to recognize me. An old man like that should never drink it."

"Is there any special name for it?"

"Just tea," Dumont said with no attempt at humor. "I drink it only in the morning or when I am on a long, hard journey and must go without sleep. There is plenty of bear meat left, plus bacon and duck eggs. We may go hungry before this trouble is over, but it hasn't happened yet. What would you like?"

Hardesty came in without knocking. For a moment, his lanky frame was outlined in the cold bright sunshine that came in the doorway. The earflaps of a beaver hat were pulled down over his ears, and his red face was raw from the wind. He clapped his gloved hands together and stomped the snow from his knee-high laced boots.

He was in better humor than he had been the night before. He had probably decided to take a new tack, but

Sundance felt the enmity in the man.

Hardesty sniffed the air in the cabin. "Taking your morning medicine, are you, Gabriel?"

"Shut the door," Dumont growled and drank a full cup of the bad-smelling concoction. Quickly, he drank a second cup. "Did you come here on business?"

"That I did, so let your breakfast wait till later. Louis wants you to come over right away. Bring the prisoner, he says."

"Did Nolin arrive?"

"Nolin's here. Got here early this morning. So did Ouellette, Duman and Isbister. There won't be any backing off now. I tell you, I feel good this morning."

To Sundance the names meant nothing, but to the *métis* they were names from the past, from the days of Riel's first rebellion. Hardesty went out whistling; Dumont looked after him with a sour expression.

"We'd better go," he said.

After they had bundled up and walked over to Riel's cabin, Hardesty had left. Riel, wearing a shaggy fur coat that fell to his ankles, sat by the fire, drinking coffee. Under his eyes there were dark rings that looked like bruises. Sundance wondered if he had slept at all since the night before. Except for two empty egg shells on the table, there was no sign he had eaten.

Dumont looked around. "Where are they? The Irishman said Nolin and the others were here?"

Riel said, "They have gone to the Lindsay schoolhouse south of Prince Charles. It is the best place to hold a meeting. More people than we knew of will be coming. Such a response encourages and yet saddens me. Ah, well, we shall see what happens."

Sundance found Riel staring at him. After a long silence, Riel said, "I have decided. You can stay. Hardesty is still against letting you join us. He does not want you in his ranks, so you will go with Gabriel. Is that all right with you, Gabriel?"

Dumont shrugged. "I don't mind."

Riel said, "I am trusting you, Sundance. I hope there will be no cause to regret it." He smiled. "You would be paid if you served with Hardesty. He has money to pay his men. The rest of us, the halfbreeds"—suddenly they all smiled—"must soldier without pay. We fight for food and freedom. Soon there may not be much of either. Now let us ride and listen to the speeches." Riel looked from Dumont to Sundance. "Gabriel hates speeches."

"What is there to speech about, Louis? We're gathering to fight. So do we fight or make speeches? If we wait too long, we'll still be making speeches when the Mounties and the militia march in on us. Regina is where the Canadians will group their forces, because the railroad from the east comes through there. But don't forget, there are Mountie barracks in Prince Albert, Battleford, and Fort Pitt. There are few men, but they are there."

Riel's escort of one-hundred halfbreeds was drawn up in the wide space between the barracks. A ragtag army, by the standards of any country, just like the Confederates, the worst-disciplined soldiers in the world. As they rode along in front of the ranked horsemen, Sundance realized for the first time how much of a fight the Canadians were in for. In all the faces, young and old, there was the same go-to-hell look of defiance; they sat their horses with careless ease. One and all, they were halfbreeds, and they ranged from almost full-blooded Indians to blue-eyed men like Sundance himself. If they had officers of any kind, it didn't show; nobody wore a uniform or insignia. Nobody saluted anyone else.

When they reached the head of the column, all Dumont did was raise his hand and they moved out to the north. Sundance could see that, unlike the others, Riel was not a very good horseman. He sat the animal properly enough, but there was none of the grace that belonged to Dumont and the others.

Their breath steamed in the morning cold; there had been an ice storm recently, and the trees were still sheathed in ice, some of the branches broken by the weight.

The village of Batoche, mostly cabins, straggled for a mile or two along the river. At the center of the settlement was a ferry, known as Batoche Crossing. Here, a few stores of log and frame hugged the riverbank. From the ferry, a path about a mile long led up to the crest of the river valley. That crest was crowned by the church, with the parish house across from it. Six miles upstream there was another ferry.

"Gabriel owns that ferry," Riel said. "It is even named after him. After that, it isn't too long to ride to the Lindsay schoolhouse. I chose it for two reasons. It is centrally placed, and there are many English halfbreeds in the Prince Albert region. They are fine people in their own way, but like all people they are different. Like us, they want to be left in peace. We are stronger than they are, so they know that if we are defeated, they might as well move beyond the maps. There will be no hope for them. They are inclined to make common cause with us, but they aren't sure they can trust us. They are Protestant and we are Catholic. Religious rivalry has always been the curse of the Territories, as it has in Canada."

Dumont had been listening. Now and then he looked at Sundance. When they were a mile from the second ferry, he sent a party of riders on ahead to look out for the possibility of an ambush.

Riel asked, "Did you know that I want to start a new church in the Territories?" Suddenly he laughed. "I can see by your face that the answer is yes. And when you heard or read about it, you thought I was mad, a mad

60

messiah with not only his own country but his own church. And if I had a crown, I could be king or emperor."

"Well," Sundance said, "both churches you mentioned have been around for a long time. People are sort of attached to them."

"They have been around too long. Religion as we know it has caused the death of more people than all the plagues. Here in the Territories I am going to change that. I am going to try. Religion brings people together or tears them apart. Here in North America, the Catholics and Protestants have been at each other's throats for more than a century. I see no hope for peace until there is one true church. A new church, a new country."

They reached the ferry and crossed the broad river. Sundance was thinking. When you began to know a man, many things you heard about him in the past and didn't understand made sense. There was no way of knowing how this new church idea would work out, but it was a bold stroke. From a political viewpoint, it had some chance of success.

On the other side of the river, they stopped at the snow-covered cabin of an ancient halfbreed with a leathery face and no teeth. Bowing, he invited them to come in, but Dumont said there wasn't time. The old halfbreed hurried into the cabin and came out with cups of bark tea. It was boiling hot and had a pleasant smell in the still air.

The old man stood and waved after them until they were out of sight. Not much more than an hour later the tall, white-painted frame building of the Lindsay schoolhouse was in sight. The road leading to it was well guarded. The schoolhouse stood on a hill. On all sides of it were tethered horses, buckboards, spring wagons, and sleighs. Horses pawed the ground and half-wild dogs ran back and forth, barking with excitement. In the churchlike tower of the schoolhouse, a man with field glasses scanned the countryside. There were hundreds of people there, both inside and outside the school. Before long, the figure would pass a thousand and keep climbing. Still they kept coming, trailing down from the hills, from out of the frozen swamps, by dogsled on the ice-hard river. Among the crowd were Indians and a handful of whites, long settled in the Territories.

Riel was smiling with satisfaction. "Look at them, Sundance," he exulted. "My people are answering the call. This time it won't be what it was in 1869. We were poorly organized then, no money, no friends. The halfbreeds are finally having their day. Don't tell me you are not moved by it!"

Sundance nodded. At the same time, he was thinking that these poor people, brave though they were, didn't have a chance. Among them, there were many who had never seen a train. Most knew little of the outside world, the tricks of politicians, the deviousness of men like Colum Hardesty. They lived in a world where all that mattered was family and honor; where a promise once given had to be kept. Yes, he was moved by their faith. For the moment, that was all he knew.

A loud cheer rang out when the crowd at the schoolhouse saw the column of horsemen coming along the south road. Hundreds of men snatched off their hats and caps and waved them in the air. A small band of musicians with miscellaneous instruments blared on the steps of the school. Riel's bodyguard dropped away, and he rode in, a vulnerable-looking figure in the full-length fur coat. Children threw handmade paper flowers in front of his horse's feet. The bell in the tower began to peal. Sundance looked up; the man with the field glasses had his hands pressed over his ears.

Hardesty stood on the steps with another man, who looked Irish. General Crook had mentioned two other Irishmen, Cunningham and Lane, in his report, but there had been no descriptions. It could be either one. The Fenians were a dangerous bunch all right; their favorite sport was to kill prominent politicians who didn't agree with them. They were mixed up in dirty business from Central America to Hudson Bay. In Mexico, they were giving aid to the rebels because President Diaz was too friendly with the powerful British mining companies. During the Civil War, they had tried to blow up Confederate warships being built in British seaports. Sundance knew the blood of innocent people had no meaning for them.

Riel dismounted awkwardly, hampered by his long coat. One of Dumont's men ran to grab the reins, and the crowd cheered the horse as it was led away. Dumont good naturedly pushed people aside as Riel walked up the steps of the schoolhouse. Now and then, Riel stopped to speak to a child or an old man; there was a cheer every time he did. At the top of the steps, he shook hands with Hardesty and the other Irishman. The two Irishman looked at Sundance with blank faces, and he knew they had been talking about him.

"We can't get any more in," Hardesty said. "The place has been packed for an hour. We'd better go in. Nolin and the others are waiting."

Riel raised his hand. "In a moment, Colum. Some of these people have come a long way, and the day is cold." Turning on the steps, he spoke to the crowd gathered in front and on both sides:

"I am sorry, my people, but there is no more room inside. But I don't want you to return to your homes. I want you to remain here. By doing so, you will give me your support. News of what is going on inside will be given to you. Today, my people, we are going to decide what must be done if we are to be free. All our leaders are present today, all gathered together for the first time. There will be speeches." Riel made a face and the crowd laughed. "But when all the talking is done, the hard decision still has to be made. You know what that is!"

With the applause of the crowd roaring behind him, Riel walked into the schoolhouse, followed by Dumont, Sundance, Hardesty, and the second Irishman. The thin wooden walls that partitioned the various classrooms had been taken out, so now there was one huge room. The desks had been taken out, too. All that remained was a long table supported by iron trestles on a raised platform at the back of the room. In front of the platform was another table for lesser dignitaries. Many of the seats at both tables were already occupied.

None of the faces meant anything to Sundance. He noted that two of the men were priests; neither looked satisfied with the proceedings. The big room was filled to capacity with men and some women; no children were present. Damp clothes steamed in the heat of several hundred bodies packed together. An officious looking elderly man, who might have been a lawyer's clerk if not for his copper skin, made a fuss about opening some of the windows. There were no benches in the room. Some people remained standing, but most had settled down on the muddy floor. Several had brought food, for they had been told it was going to be a long day.

The crowd made way for Riel, and he walked directly to the platform. The men there rose to greet him, some with the warmth of old friendship, some with reserve. Sundance noticed that one of the two priests did not shake hands with Riel. The priest who shook his hand was lean and quick-eyed, in his middle thirties; the other cleric was an old man with a stocky build and a great mane of white hair.

The hand shaking and hugging went on for a while. Sundance wondered where it was all going to lead. If it went far enough, it would lead many people there to death. But, Sundance decided, few if any of the men on the platform would die. That was how it worked. The politicians made rousing speeches and the foot soldiers died.

Among the men on the platform there was an uneasiness. From time to time, their eyes darted to the two empty chairs, then to the door. Sundance stood with his back to the wall, watching while Hardesty whispered something to Gabriel Dumont. After that, Riel whispered to Dumont. Both times Dumont shook his head.

There was more whispering. Finally, Riel took out a large silver watch, opened the face cover, and put it on the table in front of him. He was about to speak when, suddenly, there was a commotion outside the church. He leaned over to speak to Dumont, who sat beside him, and this time the big halfbreed nodded. Riel smiled, Dumont did not.

Riel raised his voice until it could be heard clearly in every corner of the big room. "Our Indian brothers are here," he said. "As soon as they have been made welcome, this meeting—this convention—will begin."

The crowd remained silent, almost fearful, while two Indians came in the door and walked toward the platform. Both were big men; the older one was handsome and looked intelligent. Sundance recognized them as Crees, tribesmen of great ferocity at one time and, from all reports, becoming increasingly hostile to the whites on both sides of the border. Looking at the two Cree chiefs, Sundance could well understand General Crook's fear of an all-out Indian war in the North West. In the Territories alone, there were twenty-thousand fighting Indians: Plains and Woods Cree, Blackfeet, Assiniboin, Stoney, runaway Sioux from Montana, and others. There had been little of the savage Indian fighting in the Territories that had plagued the States; but as the buffalo died out and food grew scarce, hatred was beginning to simmer. Then there was the matter of manhood. The warlike Sioux, still boasting of their victory over Custer nine years before, taunted the Cree's and the others as "tame" Indians and "old women." That alone would be enough to start trouble.

The two Indians stopped in front of the platform, and Riel reached down to shake hands with them. It was all done with great dignity. Then they sat in the two empty seats and folded their arms across their chests. Sundance looked at their faces and saw nothing but masks. He wondered what they were thinking; there was no way to tell.

Louis Riel stood up and raised both hands above his head. His voice was shaking with emotion when he spoke:

"Let us begin."

Nine

First, Riel introduced the men on the platform. "You know some of them, my people. Everyone knows Gabriel Dumont, good Gabriel of the rough tongue and the good heart. If war with the Canadians must come, Gabriel will lead our men. Does anyone object?"

The crowd thundered its applause. Riel nodded and motioned the people to be quiet. "That is good," he went on. "I am your leader. I returned from exile because you sent for me, but I rule only with your consent. If at any time you are displeased with my leadership, then you must tell me. I will step aside in favor of a better man."

The crowd roared, "No! No!"

Riel was very good, Sundance thought. Maybe he was a little too good. He was playing the crowd like a melodeon, squeezing out the notes and watching them dance. But that's what all politicians, even honest ones, did or tried to do. It was a tricky trade, no matter how you looked at it.

Next, Riel introduced the two priests, though everyone knew who they were. Sundance knew that, in a French-Canadian community, the priests should have come before Dumont. Riel, the politician, was making a point no one there could miss. The priests were in a place of honor at the meeting—only as long as they didn't get in the way.

Riel spoke their names: Father André and Father Grandin. Both men nodded. The old one with the white hair was Father André. Grandin, the priest who was eager to please Riel, smiled nervously and half rose from his chair.

Then the other men were introduced: Charles Nolin—"my cousin"—Riel said to loud applause. Moise Ouellette, Michel Dumas, James Isbister. And there were others.

Riel said, "These men have been with me from the beginning. Through the years, we have been harried by the police and insulted in the newspapers. At one time, an attempt was made on the life of Michel Dumas. They say the Mounties always get their man, but somehow they let this one get away—because, of course, he was known by certain men in the Canadian government. Michel still carries the bullet, a reminder of Canadian democracy in action."

After Riel let the crowd laugh for a while, he protested, "It isn't funny. Michel's only crime was that he talked too freely in the name of freedom. Yes, my people, for more than fifteen years they have been trying to stop us. Petitions, genuine letters of complaint, have been sent and never received—so they say—and always never answered. And when there is some sort of response, it is unfailingly the same: Be patient! Trust the good men in government! Trust in John A. Macdonald, Prime Minister of the glorious Dominion of Canada! Soon, everything will be wonderful! All you have to do is wait!"

Riel raised his fist. "Do you want to wait?"

Looking at the excited faces turned toward the speaker, once again Sundance decided that Louis Riel knew his business. His voice was clear and deep, but it was his hands the crowd watched, fascinated by the way he used them. All Frenchmen used their hands when they talked. Riel had gone far beyond the usual gestures; maybe he had practiced this spellbinding, and maybe it was natural. It didn't matter. The effect on the crowd was the same.

Continuing after the noise died down, Riel said: "For more than fifteen years we have been patient. Is that not long enough? Now the Canadian Pacific Railroad is complete, and the government in Ottawa has plans to bury us under tens of thousands of immigrants. Not just Scots and English and Irish, but Germans, Russians, and Swedes—people who do not know our ways and would despise them if they did. If we wait any longer, it will be like trying to fight a plague of locusts. And like the locusts in the Bible, they will fill the land until they occupy every square inch of it. When that happens, there will no longer be any chance for a *métis* nation. Instead of living as free men and women, you will be crowded off your land.

"For some of you it has already happened. And how will you live then? I will tell you how. The men will work as hired hands, slaving from dawn to dust, on farms across which their ancestors roamed freely. There will be no more joy in life, nothing but these sour-faced Scotchmen with their hellfire hymns. And, men, if you don't work on their farms—*their* farms, mind you—you will be forced to load their wagons, sweep out their stores, or break your backs in their lumber camps and mines. And what about your women and children? I will tell you..."

Beating on the table and raising his eloquent voice as the moment demanded, Louis Riel continued to stir up the crowd. Some of the other men at the table were given a chance to speak, but it was clear that Riel's talk of out-and-out rebellion frightened some of them. It frightened James Isbister, the English halfbreed from Prince Albert, a skinny sallow-faced man with the nervous habit of coughing after every few words. He argued that freedom, or at least partial independence, could be gained without bloodshed. First, he said, they had to show the Canadians how determined they were. On the other hand, they had to move cautiously.

Some man in the crowd who knew Isbister yelled, "You say that because you have more to lose than we have. You are a townsman with a hardware store. What do you know about the land or what it is to be really free?"

Michel Dumas, the man who had been wounded, was even more extreme than Riel. His dark eyes glittered with hatred, his knobby fists clenching and unclenching as he spoke:

"The time has come to wash the Saskatchewan Valley in blood. There is no other way. They call us stupid, dirty, careless. We are half starved now because we wiped out the buffalo in our stupidity. Serves us right, they say, so we should be glad to eat their salt bacon instead of real meat. But what about the railroad? Everyone knows the railroad wiped out the buffalo. The buffalo will not cross a railroad track unless driven over it by fire. So the herds were split into north and south, divided and scattered. They talk of our stupidity! And I will say now what I have often said before: The Canadians don't just want to control us. They want to exterminate us!"

A wild roar went up from the crowd. Sundance noticed that Riel stood up quickly, as if to prevent any more firebrand outbursts from Dumas. He was getting too much attention. No clever politician could let that happen. Sundance knew Riel was going to say something that would startle and infuriate the crowd.

His voice was low and penetrating: "My people, I do not know if they want to exterminate us, as Michel says, but I do know they want to get rid of me. Wait! Wait! Let me continue. Most of you know who D. H. MacDowall is—a powerful man in the Territories, a man who would like to become even more powerful. When I first returned from Montana, word came to me that MacDowall wanted to have a meeting with me. I refused. I know MacDowall and have never had any reason to trust him. I did not think there was anything to discuss. Another messenger came, and again I refused." Riel paused. "Then a third go-between came to me. I will not reveal his name, but he is in this room at this very moment. Wait! I will not reveal his name because I leave what he did—tried to do—to his own conscience. This great friend of our people said MacDowall and his friends—meaning, I suppose, the Canadian government—were willing to pay me one-hundred-thousand dollars in cash on condition that I leave the Territories, never to return. Think about it, my people, one-tenth of a million dollars just to get rid of a poor schoolteacher!"

Riel spoke quickly now. "Do you have any idea how much money that it? I am what they call an educated man, and it is almost beyond my understanding."

Finally, the shouting faded. Riel said: "I have worked as a store clerk and a prairie schoolteacher, and for several years I roamed with the buffalo hunters of Montana and Wyoming. I have never had more than two-hundred dollars at once in my life."

He laughed. "And I thought myself rich when I had that much. But one-hundred-thousand dollars! My God! the figure danced in front of my eyes! And do you think I was tempted?"

The crowd roared, "No!"

Riel smiled slyly, as though taking them into his confidence. "Yes," he said, "I was tempted. You don't want to think your leader is a fool, do you?"

The crowd remained silent.

"For about ten seconds I was tempted," Riel shouted,

"and then I told MacDowall's emissary to go back and tell his master the answer was no. Not for a million and not for ten million!"

Father André stood up shakily. The crowd stopped yelling and stared at him, unsure of what he was about to say. Riel's dark eyes flickered from face to face. It was very quiet in the big room.

"I am the man Louis is talking about," the old priest began. He waited for the yelling to start again, but there was only silence. "MacDowall is not my master. Only God is my master, and I serve Him willingly. When Louis first returned from Montana, I welcomed him because I know how much you have suffered and how much you respect him. Louis is back, I thought, and he is fifteen years older, not so hotheaded as he was. He has been a schoolteacher, is married, with a wife and two daughters in Montana. He is even an American citizen. We talked, and at first I like what he had to say. Then, as weeks and months passed, I saw that he was more hotheaded than ever."

Michel Dumont started to say something. Riel silenced him immediately: "Let the friend of the people speak."

Father André said, "I began to see nothing but bloodshed ahead. I still do. When I heard of MacDowall's plan, I went to him; he did not come to me. I thought it would be best for everybody if Louis went back to Montana. I knew he would talk to me if not to MacDowall. I was empowered to offer him five-thousand dollars if he left the Territories. Louis said he would leave for nothing less than one-hundred thousand."

"Lying priest!" Michel Dumas shouted. "You always take the side of the rich!"

Sundance's eyes narrowed as he looked over at Riel, who was taking it calmly. Father André remained on his feet, badly shaken by the ordeal. Disregarding him completely, Riel stood up, saying, "Hold your tongue,

Michel. He is still a priest. However, in the interest of truth—not to dirty his name but to clear mine—I would like to ask him if it's true that D.H. MacDowall has promised to build him a new church and parish house?"

Father André's voice faltered. "That was months before."

Riel turned quickly and shouted like a prosecuting attorney, "Why would a Scotch Presbyterian want to build a Catholic church for the *métis*? Why would a Scotch Presbyterian want to do *anything* for the *métis*?"

Sundance knew that the crowd was squarely on Riel's side, and he knew the whole thing had been carefully planned.

The old priest held out both hands toward the sullen crowd. "Mr. MacDowall is a good man, a kind man. He came to the Territories as a poor boy from Scotland. He became rich here and wants only good for everyone here. When the Indians left the reservation and were starving, Mr. MacDowall fed them with his own beef. A wagonload of blankets was provided."

Michel Dumas, the priest-hater, was up on his feet again. "We all know that story. You know damn well the only reason MacDowall fed the Indians was to keep them from raiding his herds and his storehouses. He bought your trickery with the promise of a church. What is the cost of a church? I don't know, but a man like MacDowall would carry enough money to build it in his pocket. But your worst lie is when you said MacDowall tried to bribe Louis with a miserable five thousand. Answer me, priest. How much money would you say the North West Territories are worth? How many hundreds of millions of dollars? And you say MacDowall could spare only five thousand!"

Dumas turned to the crowd. "We know the Scotch are tight with their money. But only five thousand for a whole country!"

Riel slammed his hand on the top of the table. He continued to thump the table until there was absolute silence. "That will be enough, Michel. I do not want to hear any more about it. If this disruption could have been prevented, I would not have mentioned it at all."

Suddenly, Riel's voice rose almost to a scream. "I will allow no man, priest or not, to accuse me of treachery to my people. Because, my friends, honor is all we have. The world outside our borders is trying to destroy us, suppress our customs, push us aside as old fashioned and primitive. To hell with the rest of the world is what I say!"

Riel's voice became quiet, almost sad. "I don't want the world to go to hell. I just want it to keep out of the North West Territories." He raised his arms as if trying to hug everyone there. "We are all we have. That is why we must remain faithful to one another in all things. Without honor, there is nothing. In my mind I see a great host of enemies arrayed against us. To prevail over these destroyers, we must be strong as never before in our long history."

Riel made a grasping motion, as if picking up a handful of soil. Everybody watched his hand as he held it out toward them, his fist clenched tightly. "This—this is *our* land," he said quietly. "This is where our fathers have lived since before men can remember. Out there, the bones of our ancestors lie buried. Land, my people, is not just something you use to make a living. If that is all you think of the land, you might as well run a little dry goods store. No, the land is mother to us all. It gives us life, and we water it with our blood, fertilize it. Yes, that is the word—and with our bodies when we die. By the God that made us all, they are not going to take it away from us!"

Riel sat down as calmly as if he hadn't been ranting a moment before. Sundance thought Riel glanced over his way, but he couldn't be sure. On Riel's face there was a half smile. No, not a smile but a strange, twisted expression. His eyes looked at the crowd, but Sundance wasn't sure he saw anything but his inner thoughts.

The crowd was still yelling and stomping their feet when the old priest got up shakily and left the platform. He was infirm and trembling, but no one helped him to step down to the floor. Well, Sundance thought, he really put the boot to you today.

The crowd made a lane for the old priest to pass through. He walked slowly, eyes fixed directly in front of him. Sundance knew nothing about Father André but figured he had served this people most of his life. In the remote settlements, a priest arrived when he was young and remained until he died. How many births and deaths had this old priest presided over? Hundreds? Thousands.

Louis Riel, very calm now, waited until Father André was gone before he spoke again. It was obvious the crowd was uneasy. In the halfbreed settlement, isolated by distance and choice, a priest wasn't just a psalmsinger dressed in black. He was a living bridge between this life and the hereafter.

Yep, Sundance thought, old Louis knows his stuff. He slipped in the knife and turned it without getting even a spot of blood on his hands. Michel Dumont had done all the tough talking, while Riel had remained regretful and forgiving. How much did it have to do with Riel's new church, his "true" religion, as he called it? It probably had a lot to do with it. And what about the two stories—of the five and the hundred-thousand dollars?

In the end, it didn't matter a damn. Sundance had been sent to stop Riel. Thus far, he hadn't even begun to form a plan. All he could do at the moment was look and listen and keep Hardesty and his Irish friends from killing him. He knew they were going to try. It was in their faces every time they looked at him. He would have to tread carefully if he wanted to stay alive. He couldn't make up his mind about Riel. At times, he sounded like the world's most honorable man. But it was all shot through with trickery and deceit. Whatever he was, and he was probably many things, Louis Riel was no ordinary man. It could even be that he was an honorable man who felt he had to act like a trickster to get the things he wanted for his people. Of course, that was the trouble with so many men of destiny. They always thought they and they alone knew what was best for the ordinary man.

Riel was talking again, this time about concessions. "My plan," he said, "is not to tell the Canadians what we will do if they don't grant concessions. My plan is to do certain things—and then ask for concessions. No matter what people say, I am willing to settle for something less than complete independence." His dark eyes were hooded. "I am ready to settle for partial independence, because that will give us more time to prepare. Yes, that would be breaking a promise, I know. But how many promises have the Canadians broken? It would take an abacus to count the number. We will take whatever they give us. We will wait and prepare and arm ourselves secretly. Then we will make more demands. And so on and so on.

"That is how it is done, my friends. It is not the way I would like to do it, but at the moment we are outnumbered, so we must fight might with guile. Every concession we get takes us one more step away from Ottawa. After a while, they will begin to see complete separation as inevitable. That is how it can be achieved. It is slow, perhaps too slow for those of you who are impatient and angry. But it is the road I would like to follow, if such is possible. If not, then we'll fight. That is what I am afraid we will have to do, and you must not think it will be easy."

Now what was Riel trying to do? Sundance wondered. Sure, that was it. He was trying to sound like a man of peace while urging the *métis* toward war. Nothing Riel had said so far proved to Sundance that the man wanted peace. All his words and actions pointed toward war. It showed in his eyes when the wild words began to flow. It showed in the way he used his hands, literally tearing Canada apart in his mind.

Michel Dumas jumped to his feet. "These Canadians will be no match for us. They are a race of storekeepers and chicken farmers. They don't know this country, and we know every inch of it. We will bury them in the muskeg, lead them into the wilderness until they are lost, starving, blinded by snow. If they come into this country, they will stay here forever!"

Riel held up his hand. "That is brave talk, Michel, but we must look at the facts. They may not come at all. Macdonald is a man who finds it hard to make up his mind. I have observed his career for many years. It is possible that he will put off doing anything, then do nothing at all. Or, being the man he is, he may postpone action for a while, thinking that his militia can recapture the Territories any time he feels like that. My God, if he only took that course! Give us a year, even six months, and we'll be strong enough to turn back any force he can send."

Gesturing toward Hardesty and the other Irishman, Riel said, "Not many of you know who these gentlemen are: Mr. Hardesty and Mr. Lane. Mr. Hardesty is going to tell you a few things you will like hearing."

Hardesty got up and moved out in front of the platform. He told them that he was an Irishman, explaining what being a Fenian meant. He said he was a Catholic and a hater of Great Britain, and therefore of the Canadian government, for what was Canada, after all, but a foreign province of Queen Victoria's?

"Men and guns are coming from the United States," said Hardesty. "Some will be here soon, and others are to follow. Given enough time, we can build an army of volunteers from the United States—men, experienced soldiers who have served in the army, veterans. They are well armed, well trained, and they know how to fight. Whereas, as Michel Dumas says, the Canadian militia are nothing but storekeepers and chicken farmers, led by pot-bellied lawyers and business.

"But," Hardesty continued, "even if they don't give us the time we need, the fight against the Canadians can still be won. What we have to do is prove to them that it isn't worth it. War costs money. The longer it goes on, the more it costs. Hit them in the pocketbooks is what we have to do. In the end, that's all they understand. Contest every inch of ground. They may think war is a gentleman's name, but we will show them otherwise. We will make the war so bloody, so costly, they will wish they never heard the name of the *métis*.

"There is this railroad with which they are supposed to destroy us. In the end, it is just wood and steel, tunnels and bridges. All these things can be destroyed. Telegraph wires can be cut, the poles burned. Towns are made of wood and can be burned with a can of coal oil and a single match. Hit them, and keep on hitting. I know this has a brutal sound, but we have to do what General Sherman did in Georgia—wage total war."

Hardesty looked sideways at Riel. "Of course, there will be no killing of prisoners. We will feed them to the best of our ability. This is the chance you waited for those long fifteen years when Louis Riel was in exile. Well, let us repay them for Louis's suffering, his years of wandering without a country. All we need is courage and determination. In years to come, you can tell your grandchildren that you were here, in the Lindsay schoolhouse, when it all began."

Hardesty sat down to polite applause. He looked disappointed. He had expected a better reception. Sundance grinned behind his hand. The *métis*, poor and largely uneducated, had plenty of everyday good sense. For all his blarney and war talk, Hardesty had failed to win them over completely. That would be at least one setback for the Irishman. But it was not to rule him out as a force in the movement.

Louis Riel stood up, still applauding the Irishman. "It's time," he said, "to talk of our friends, the Indians. I know it's been on your minds. It's time we talked about it frankly and openly."

The two Indians didn't move.

Ten

Gabriel Dumont was very silent as he and Sundance rode back to Batoche across the bleak plains that stretched away on both sides of the South Saskatchewan River. The wind blew as it did all year. This was country where it snowed all through the winter; it hardly ever rained, sometimes not for years at a time. Once the snow was gone, the ever-present wind baked the land, drying it to dust. In summer it was a sun-baked hell. They called it the Canadian Desert. You either froze or fried, and there were times when the crops withered and died for lack of water.

Dumont rode without saying a word, a dead cigar stuck in his mouth. Sundance wanted to talk but knew it would be no use. The meeting at the schoolhouse was over, and with it maybe a whole way of life was over for the *métis*. A lot of arguments had been heard and many things decided. Louis Riel had spoken of the great Indian uprising to come. He had called Poundmaker and Little Bear his "brothers and allies." Together, he said, the Indians would sweep the land of the Canadian oppressors. Both Indian chiefs spoke English, but all they did was nod several times while Riel spoke of the glorious victories to come. He said "victory" and not "slaughter." But everyone knew what he meant. The Canadians still had time to come to terms, Riel said. If the war came, would be up to them. First, Riel said, the *métis* would take several towns and hold the whites as hostages. Word would then be sent to the Canadians that if they invaded *métis* territory the hostages and towns would be destroyed.

In his fierce way, Michel Dumas wanted to start the Indian war immediately. Nolin, Riel's cousin, had opposed the war unless there was no other way. To Sundance's surprise, Dumont had opposed setting the Indians against the whites. The two Cree chiefs had showed no emotion while Dumont said:

"Can we control the Indians once they get started? To set the Indians on the warpath will bring down the fury of both the Canadians and the Americans. I am proud of my Indian blood. For generations the *métis* have been a civilized people. We have towns, churchs, schools. We have books and a newspaper, a way of life that is ours. The Indians are our brothers in the sight of God. But will they remain our brothers as the fighting goes on? Poundmaker and Little Bear are men of honor. But what of men like Wandering Spirit, who hates the *métis* as much as he hates the whites? I do not think they can control such men. This is a fight for the *métis*. Let us fight it by ourselves!"

Finally, a vote was taken, and Dumont's objections were overruled. After some words of praise for Dumont, Riel declared he would return to Montana unless the participation of the Indians was approved. Faced with that, Dumont said he would go along with the majority.

Now it was over. Dumont and Sundance were heading back to Batoche. Riel and Hardesty had stayed behind to continue the talks with the other leaders. Riel's body-guard had stayed, too.

The wind blew hard and they rode without talking. The early winter darkness was coming on fast; soon, the warmth of the watery sun would be gone. Without pausing, Dumont spat out the chewed-up cigar and put another in his mouth.

The second cigar lasted another ten miles. By then, the first ferry was in sight. Up the slope from the riverbank was the cabin where the old man had given them bark tea earlier in the day. The broad, frozen river was slate gray in the light of the setting sun. Sundance thought with longing of the sunwashed southwest: Arizona, New Mexico, Sonora.

Their shoulders were hunched against the cold as they started down the long slope toward the old man's cabin. Sundance had no idea why the cabin was there. Maybe the old man sold things to travelers coming or going from the ferry. They were not much more than a hundred yards from the cabin when two rifles opened fire at the same time. Dumont pitched off his horse without a sound. He hit the ground hard and lay still. His horse spooked and ran toward the river.

Sundance yelled and rolled off his horse. When he came up again, the Winchester was in his hand and he was behind a tree. But the two riflemen kept firing at Dumont instead of at him. A bullet furrowed its way across the top of Dumont's shoulder. Another tore a hole in the brim of his hat.

Pushing the rifle out from behind the tree, Sundance threw lead at the cabin's door and window as fast as he could lever shells. The fire from the cabin slacked off under the rain of bullets. Sundance jumped from cover, and the firing started again as he grabbed Dumont by the heels and dragged him behind a tree. Dumont cursed and groaned as his face skated across the crusted snow. A bullet blew its hot breath in Sundance's face and another sang over his head.

Dumont's face was covered with blood gushing from a head wound. He tried to get up. Sundance pushed him down in the snow and told him to stay down. "I'll get them," he said.

The light was almost gone as he edged away from Dumont. Bullets tore at him from the window and door of the cabin, the muzzle flashes red-white in the enveloping grayness. The bushwhacker in the doorway was more reckless than the other. Sundance could see his outline every time he fired. They were both armed with repeaters. The trees thinned out close to the cabin. He went down on his belly in the snow and crawled forward, waiting for a clear shot.

It came in the moment the shooter in the doorway fired twice. Sundance killed him before he could fire a third shot. The man hung onto the side of the door, moaning with pain, then he fell on his face as a blaze of rifle fire jetted from the window. It stopped. In the silence that followed, Sundance heard the clack of a loading lever.

Lying in the snow, Sundance let time and the silence gnaw on the second ambusher's nerves. Three more flashes of fire came from the window. Sundance didn't shoot back because the bullets hadn't even come close to where he was. He crawled behind a tree before he told the man to come out. The answer was a single bullet ripping into a tree three feet from where he was. After that there was no more shooting.

"Come out or I'll burn you out!" Sundance yelled. "There's only one way out, and I have it covered." Cabins in the wind-blasted northwest didn't have back doors or windows. "You have one minute before you burn."

"You won't kill me?" It was a *métis*, not a Canadian or Indian voice. "Swear to God you won't kill me."

"You haven't much time left," Sundance yelled. "Come out now. I won't kill you. Throw the rifle out the window, plus any other weapons you have."

He waited. The voice said, "I am throwing out my rifle and my knife. I have no pistol. I am throwing them now. Listen to them."

Hardly able to see, Sundance heard the weapons fall in the snow. He yelled: "With your hands stretched in front of you, the fingers laced, come out."

Sundance stood up as the man came out. There wasn't enough light to make out much more than the thick, dark clothing of an ordinary *métis* with a heavy beard and a stiff-brimmed black hat. "Keep those hands stretched out," Sundance warned. "Stretch them out till it hurts. Now, stand where you are and put your legs wide apart."

Holding the rifle at his hip, Sundance went down the slope and stopped when he was six feet away. "Turn to one side," he ordered. "Now tell me your name and who hired you to kill Gabriel Dumont. The truth or I'll blow your hands off!"

"My God!" the man said, "we did not know..."

Sundance could see well enough to blow off his left thumb. The man screamed and tried to unlace his fingers. "Hold still or you lose the other one. I said, what's your name and who hired you?"

The words came out strangled. "Theodore Parie. No one hired me. Gabriel told us to come here and watch the road to the ferry. From the ferry, is what I mean to, prevent the Canadians from surprising the meeting at Batoche. Is—is Gabriel dead? We did not know. It was getting dark. If Gabriel came, we thought it would be with Louis Riel and his bodyguard."

Sundance said, "He's dead all right, you stupid son of a bitch."

The bushwhacker was lying, but this wasn't the place to make him talk. There was no use forcing it now. There would be time enough when they got him back to Batoche. Once there, Gabriel could make good use of his white-hot skinning knife.

The bushwhacker pretended to blubber, being very emotional and French. "What have we done? I swear on my mother's grave. Kill me! I don't care. But I was just following orders."

"Your own people will have to decide," Sundance said. Suddenly, as he spoke, the man's right hand flashed up toward the back of his neck and a knife appeared in his hand. He almost made it before a bullet stopped him. A .44-40 rifle bullet hit him squarely in the face and went out the back of his head. Except for the roar of the rifle and the body falling in the snow, there was no other sound.

Gabriel Dumont was up on his knees when Sundance went back to find him. "My rifle. Let me get my rifle," he kept repeating.

"Go easy," Sundance said, lifting him by his armpits. He was glad the big buffalo hunter was able to stand, however unsteadily. It would be hell to carry a man of his size. The wind and the cold had stiffened the blood on his face and, the bleeding from the head wound had stopped. Blood soaked the back of his coat, but Sundance didn't think the wound was serious.

"Did you—did you?" he said, still dazed.

"Both of them," said Sundance. "Can you make it to the cabin?"

Dumont did his best to stand up straight. The effort was painful, but he made no sound. Sundance got him to the cabin and helped him over the dead body in the doorway. Dumont had enough strength to spit before he went through.

It was dark inside. Sundance had to strike a match before he found the old man's bunk. The old man lay dead beside it. Under his chin was a knife wound without much blood. Dumont didn't want to lie down, but he didn't fight too hard when Sundance pushed him gently. Embers still glowed in the fire. Sundance built up the fire with bark chips, then piled on logs.

There was nothing much in the cabin; a rough table, two chairs, some cooking utensils on the floor by the fire. On the wall above the bunk were two pictures; a colored print of the Virgin Mary and an engraving of Louis Riel cut from a newspaper. Both were very old. In all, not much to show for a man's lifetime.

Sundance dragged the dead man outside and left him in the snow. He was a *métis*, like the other, and somewhat older. After he brought the weapons inside, Sundance barred the door. The wind was getting colder. When a kettle of water was warm enough, he spilled it into a basin, tore up a clean flannel shirt hanging on the wall, and dabbed at the wound in Dumont's head. It wasn't serious. The bullet had split the scalp without damaging the bone. The bleeding stopped after he washed out the wound.

Behind the stack of logs, he found a half-full bottle of whisky. He poured whiskey in the wound and bandaged it tightly with a strip of flannel. Then he got Dumont's coat and shirt off and looked at the wound in his back. It was long but shallow and would be sore for a while. When he finished with the back wound, there was just enough left for two big drinks.

"Don't worry, you won't go wild," he said, holding the bottle to Dumont's lips. "There isn't enough to make you wild, not the way you're feeling. What's left is for me. How are you feeling?"

Dumont's throat worked furiously as the whiskey went down. He drank exactly half the whiskey and handed the bottled back to Sundance. "I'm all right," he said. "A little man with a big drum is beating time in my head."

"I'll bet he is. Can you see all right? Do what I do."

Sundance stretched out his arm, then touched his nose with his index finger.

There was a deep growl of protest. "Damn foolishness!"

"Do it, Gabriel. Later you can complain all you want."

Looking sour, Dumont touched his finger to his nose. "That whiskey is as bad as mine," he said.

Sundance drank what was left in the bottle and didn't think it was any worse than Dumont's. It might even have been a little better. "I guess you'll be all right," he said. "We'll rest here for a while, then start back to Batoche."

"I can start back now."

"In a while, I said."

Dumont raised himself on his elbow, his forehead creased with a massive headache. "Who's in command here?"

Sundance said, "Right now, I am. Those two men I killed, you didn't post them here? They were *métis*."

"Not *métis*. Men dressed as *métis*."

"They were *métis*. And they knew you'd be coming back alone."

"Hardesty!" Dumont's dark eyes were dark with sudden anger.

"That's right," Sundance said. "The meeting was over, and we were getting ready to leave when Hardesty told Riel there were other things, important things, to talk about. Riel told you to go ahead and to take me with you."

"Oh, not Louis. Why would he?"

"I didn't say that. Maybe it was something Hardesty said about me. They had been talking; I couldn't hear them."

"I'll kill him," Dumont said quietly, touching the bandage on his head.

Sundance wasn't about to plead for the Irishman's life, but he didn't want to agree too quickly. "You have no proof it was Hardesty who planned this."

The big buffalo hunter thumped his chest. "In my heart I have proof. In my head—especially in my head—I have proof. I knew it would always come to something like this. To killing. But I thought he would face me like a man."

"One of the men said his name was Theodore Parie. Do you know him?"

"That dog! He is one of the Montana *métis*. We heard he had escaped from prison after having been sent there with others for robbing a bank. When he came here, he swore he had done it to get money for the cause. Another *métis* of the same gang came with him. The other man you killed?"

Sundance described him.

"Elzear Bedard," Dumont said. "They were always together." Dumont smiled viciously. "Now they are together in death. In their pockets I think you will find American money. Thieves, killers, now dead assassins. I never believed their story about the bank robbery." Dumont shrugged. "But we need men and still do."

It was hard for a man like Dumont to express gratitude. "You saved my life, Sundance. They were shooting at me. You could have ridden off and left me."

"Where would I go?"

"Back to the schoolhouse."

"They'd think I killed you."

"That was not the reason. Never will I forget what you did today," Dumont said.

"If you can talk so much, you should be able to travel," Sundance said. "If you fight as good as you talk, you'll have the Canadians whipped in no time."

Dumont grinned in spite of his throbbing skull. "Go to hell, halfbreed."

Sundance grinned back. "Look who's calling me a halfbreed!" he said. "Now you rest easy while I go catch your horse."

He found the animal, quiet now, down by the edge of the river. What sounded like pistol shots came from the middle of the river as the thinner ice broke up. There was a channel of clear water where the ferry crossed. He led Dumont's horse back to the cabin and tied it to a tree.

Then he roped the two dead men after searching their pockets where he found a fifty-dollar bill on each body. Next, he dragged them down to the river and dumped them into the channel. The current took them under the ice. It would be weeks before all the ice broke up, months before they floated downstream to Batoche.

Back again at the cabin, he collected the spent shells and put them in his pocket. Dumont looked at him curiously as he rolled the old man's body under the bunk and pushed it out of sight.

"What are you doing, Sundance?"

"I think you ought to surprise Hardesty when he gets back to Batoche. See! Nobody got killed here. There was no shooting. Hardesty will wonder what happened to you. You sure you can travel?"

Dumont thumped his chest, a thing he did often. "I am as strong as I ever was."

"Good," said Sundance. "Then you'll be able to fix the duck eggs and ham you were bragging about this morning."

Eleven

There were fifty prisoners under heavy guard when they got back to Batoche. Fires blazed in the streets of the village and across the river in the encampment. Sundance and Dumont saw the fires from miles upriver. The old man who took them across on the ferry was shaking with excitement.

"We have captured a whole army of Canadians, a whole army," he said. "They came with horses and wagons and guns. Not a shot was fired. Our men trapped them on the road from the south."

Canadians! Dumont looked at Sundance. It didn't make any sense.

In front of the barracks fifty men sat huddled in the wind, watched by two *métis* behind the Gatling gun. Rifelmen guarded them on the other side. The wagons and horses of the captured men were standing some distance away.

Men came running when they saw Dumont, but the cheering stopped when they saw the bloody bandage around his head. Dumont roared at them to be quiet when they started yelling.

Sundance and Dumont dismounted and walked over

to the *métis* in charge of the prisoners. "You, Garneau," said Dumont, "what is all this?"

"Their leader says they came to fight with Hardesty, the Irishman. I do not believe them."

Dumont swore furiously. "More Hardestys," he said. "Which one is the leader?"

"The one standing up with the red hair in the caped greatcoat. He says his name is O'Neal."

"What the hell do you think you're doing?" O'Neal demanded when Garneau brought him over. "Who are you and where the hell is Hardesty? We didn't come a thousand miles, dodging the Mounties, to be treated like this. Senator Niles in New York is going to hear about this."

"He is lying," Garneau whispered.

"Go away!" Dumont roared.

O'Neal was still outraged. "My men are freezing out here. If we are to be prisoners, then treat us like soldiers." The redheaded Irishman looked like an ex-cavalryman to Sundance, probably a good one too. He wore wire-rimmed spectacles that took nothing away from his military bearing. An empty holster was strapped to his broad leather belt.

"Can you prove who you are?" Dumont was not impressed with the other man's anger. "A paper, a letter."

O'Neal said, "I have a safe conduct pass with Hardesty's signature on it. I showed it to your man, but I don't know if he can read."

"He can read French, his own language." Dumont said, unfolding the paper. After he read it, he gave it to Sundance. "It looks like Hardesty's signature. Look at the fancy way he writes his name.

"I see he's made himself a colonel," Sundance said. Colonel Hardesty—the noncom in the British Army had come a long way in a few years. Among the Fenians there were more colonels than in the Mexican army.

Dumont kept the safe conduct pass. "My apologies," he said, not sorry at all, "but you arrived early. Hardesty said the first men wouldn't arrive until the end of the week."

O'Neal said with a sneer, "We should have taken our time, but I thought there was a war to be fought. Next time we won't be so prompt."

His sarcasm was lost on Dumont, who said, "Next time I think you better stay in New York. But you're here, and your men will need food and shelter. Garneau did not make them sit here for nothing." Dumont called Garneau. "See that these men are quartered and fed. Join your men, Mr. O'Neal."

"I am Major O'Neal."

"Be anything you like. Join your men."

To Garneau, Dumont said, "Turn the Gatling gun around and move it back. You had it too close to them. If they had attacked, you would have had no chance to use it. Don't make the same mistake again. Guard them well. There may be trouble with Hardesty."

Dumont told Garneau to go away when he asked about his head. "And put out those damned fires! I don't want Mr. Hardesty to get excited when he rides in. No one has seen me. Do you understand?"

Garneau didn't understand, but he nodded.

"Give them the best food we have," Dumont ordered. "No slop. These men are our *friends*. But don't give them whiskey." Dumont smiled at Sundance. "Irishmen are worse than Indians."

When they got to the cabin, Sundance wanted Dumont to rest. "Then who will cook the ham and duck eggs?" Dumont asked. "You have eaten duck eggs?"

Sundance had to admit not lately. "Well, they're here, the first of them are," he said and stretched out on his bunk, while Dumont greased a skillet. "What do you think?"

"I think duck eggs have to be fried right, or they taste like rubber. About the Irishmen? I don't know what I think. This one called O'Neal looks all right. I don't know about the others, but they brought a Gatling gun. Now we have two."

"The Canadians have more than that."

"I know," Dumont said, turning away.

They were eating when horseman thundered into the encampment. Shouting started and stopped. Dumont swigged down the last of his tea and put his Winchester on the table. Sundance eased the Colt in his oiled holster. The door opened and Riel came in, followed by Hardesty.

"Gabriel! They said you were wounded," Riel said. "Did you see the man—the men—who did it?"

So much for the surprise, Sundance thought, watching Hardesty instead of Riel. Hardesty didn't miss the rifle on the table. He didn't speak because Riel was asking the questions.

"Sundance saw them and killed them, Louis. They were Theodore Parie and Elzear Bedard, two good *métis* from Montana. Each man had fifty American dollars in his pocket. They had no money when they came here from jail, just the ragged clothes on their backs."

Riel passed his hand over his face and sat down. "But this is unthinkable. Two of our own people took money to kill you? Where are they now?"

"In the river," Sundance said, still watching Hardesty.

Hardesty was a quick thinker. "Maybe the Canadians made a deal with them while they were in jail and bribed the jailers to let them escape."

"That won't wash," Sundance said. "Why would they try to kill Gabriel? Louis is the man to kill."

Without looking up, Riel said piously, "I am not the whole movement."

Dumont stood up, almost knocking over the table. "They were paid by someone closer to home I think. I will speak plainly. You could have hired them, Hardesty. I say you *did* hire them."

Hardesty's hand jerked toward his gun, but Sundance knew he wasn't going to draw it. It was the Irishman's way of showing how shocked and angry he was. Dumont's hand was on the rifle. If Hardesty had tried for a draw, Sundance would have killed him before his hand had touched the butt of the gun.

"Please, my friends!" Riel got between them with outstretched hands—the man of peace. "This is what they want, to have us quarrel. There has to be some explanation."

"Hardesty wants to get rid of me, Louis."

"Louis, why would I want to do that? I lead my men, Gabriel leads his."

Dumont said, "I lead all the men. That was the plan."

"That was the plan, Gabriel." Riel seemed to be speaking in the past tense. So it seemed to Sundance.

"Even if you were dead, the *métis* would never follow me," Hardesty argued.

Sundance knew the *métis* would follow anyone Riel told them to.

"But you have no proof, Gabriel," Riel said. "Did the men talk? They didn't accuse anyone?"

"They would have, Louis. If they were alive, they would talk." Dumont touched the haft of the skinning knife. "They would have told everything."

Riel shook his head. "But they aren't alive. The American money you found was just American money."

"And who has the most American money in Batoche?"

"Certainly I don't, Gabriel. Mr. Hardesty has the most American money. Would you condemn a man for having a lot of money? But I have *some* American money. Why don't you accuse me? We argued today in public, so I became angry at your insubordination and paid Parie and Bedard to kill you. Simple, is it not?"

"Bah!" Gabriel Dumont said.

"Of course it's foolish, Gabriel, but I could have done it. You are wounded, and you are angry, and you want to blame Mr. Hardesty because you don't like him."

"I don't give a damn if he likes me or not, Louis. You want to see how much money I have, Dumont? I'll show you." The Irishman took a thick leather-clasped wallet from inside his coat and snapped it open. It was stuffed with money in big bills. "See, Dumont, American money, Canadian money, even English pound notes. You think that's all the proof you need? You know what I think? I think you don't want to admit that two of your own people tried to murder you. Those two men didn't belong to me. They belonged to you. I didn't know them, and I didn't send for them."

Riel shrugged. "What he says is true, Gabriel. They were your men, your responsibility."

The Irishman sensed that he had the advantage now. "I don't give a damn if you believe me or not. We can settle this right now, if that's what you want. Nobody interferes. Just you and me."

Brave, Sundance thought, very brave! Challenging a badly shaken man who ought to be resting in his bunk.

"No! No! This is madness!" Riel said.

"With respect, Louis," Dumont said, "this is between the Irishman and me."

Sundance stood up, his hand not far from his gun. "Maybe not," he said. "It could be just as well be between Hardesty and me. Gabriel is a little tired right now. If that bullet had been an inch or two closer, he'd be dead."

"Who says I'm tired?" Suddenly Dumont was as wild as a bull getting ready to charge.

"With respect, Gabriel," Sundance said. "Shut up! What's it going to be, Hardesty? They shot at me too. I'm almost as mad as Gabriel. How would you like it to be? It can't be pistols. You wouldn't have a chance. It can't be knives because I'd cut you to ribbons. What about fists and feet? You Irishmen are good with your fists and feet."

This time Riel didn't protest. Sundance knew then that the *métis* leader liked to see what his men were made of. There was no need to test Dumont, even if he had been in condition to fight. Riel had known him too long.

"Fine with me," Hardesty said truculently. "Now is fine with me. After you, sir." The Irishman was putting on airs again—the British Army noncom who wanted to be a gentleman. So far, nothing had been said about the fifty Fenians.

They left their weapons on the table in Dumont's cabin and went out into the snow. It was biting cold, one of the coldest days of that March of 1885. Soon they would be sweating.

"Any rules?" Hardesty asked.

"None," was the answer.

Bundled in a long fur coat with his hat pulled down over his ears, Riel came out to watch the fight.

Moving away from the cabin, Sundance and Hardesty stopped when they reached a place where the snow had been beaten down by horses. Pale moonlight filtered through the clouds. The wind was blowing steadily.

Hardesty moved with ease for a big man. He was the veteran of many brawls and knew how good he was with his fists. Sundance decided it wasn't going to be a cinch to knock him down. He was going to do his damnedest, because a man who would pay ambushers to murder a decent man had pain coming to him. 'Colonel' Hardesty would learn that he had come to the wrong place to play tin soldier.

There was a long pause while they sized one another up. Then the Irishman came at Sundance, taking his time, fists weaving, shoulders hunched. Well now, thought Sundance, Hardesty fancies himself a boxer as well as a gentleman. A fist came straight at Sundance's face and he

96

turned it aside. While he was doing it, a left thumped him hard in the ribs. Sundance punched back with his left and missed. He followed with the left again, and this time it landed—not a hard, telling blow, but one that got inside the Irishman's defense. Hardesty moved in, throwing rights and lefts but keeping the punches short so he would not be caught off balance. Sundance had one big advantage. His thick-soled but flexible north-country moccasins gripped the frozen ground, while Hardesty's heavy boots skidded.

A punch that seemed to come from nowhere rocked Sundance's head. If he hadn't jerked it aside, another would have landed in the same place. The Irishman bored in again and grunted with pain when he was stopped by a blow to the heart. Suddenly, Hardesty lowered his left and jabbed at Sundance's belly. Even though he sidestepped some of the force, the Irishman's hard fist made the halfbreed's stomach muscles tense with pain.

Both men backed off and circled one another. The sweat on their shirts was beginning to freeze. So far, there had been no kicking. The Irishman would have to start it first. Sundance knew he would.

The first kick came after Sundance nearly toppled Hardesty with a right to the jaw. He braced his feet against the force of the punch and his arms waved as he tried to regain his balance. Sundance was moving in to deliver another right when Hardesty kicked at his knee. Had the kick landed, the kneecap would have been shattered by a heavy boot powered by a muscular leg.

After dodging around the Irishman kicked again. This time it dug into Sundance's thigh. The whole leg felt as if it had been whacked with an ax handle. Hardesty followed the kick with a mad rush. Down and down he dived at Sundance's belly, trying to knock him down in the snow. Sundance let himself go with the force of the rush, then he reached up and grabbed Hardesty by both arms, and threw himself flat on his back so that his feet came up at the same time. There was a wild shout as the Irishman was thrown ten feet over Sundance's head. He landed with a crash with the wind knocked out of him and was still gasping when Sundance turned, jumped in the air, and landed with all his weight on the small of Hardesty's back. Then, jumping to one side, the halfbreed kicked the Irishman in the side, and then did it again.

Hardesty screamed and tried to get a hold on Sundance's kicking foot. He got a grip but lost it, and then he was kicked again with the other foot. The Irishman tried to roll away, but Sundance followed him with kicks. Finally, he lay on his back, holding up his hands, quivering with pain and anger.

It would have been easy for Sundance to kill him with a right kick to the temple, the weakest part of the skull. The Irishman's hands were still grabbing at nothing when Sundance drew back for that last kick.

"You want more?" Sundance yelled, still thinking of the ambush at the cabin and the old man's knife wound in his throat. "You want more? I'll give you more. But you have to say what you want."

"I've had enough," Hardesty groaned. "No more." He rolled away, and Sundance let him go, though he knew it wasn't finished. No matter what happened, from now on Hardesty would never let it drop.

Hardesty stood up, holding his ribs and trying to smile. He had a smile like a rabid wolf. Dumont watched silently. Also smiling, Riel came forward. "Enough of this stupid brawling," he said. "I want you two men to shake hands and say there is no hard feeling between you. Come on now, that is an order."

Holding out his hand, Sundance said, "I have no hard feelings." He was lying.

They shook hands.

"None here," Hardesty said. He too was lying.

"Good! Good!" Louis Riel declared. "We will attack the day after tomorrow."

Twelve

That same night, in the Parliament Buildings in Ottawa, lights were burning late. All day long, messengers from the telegraph office on the fourth floor had been running up and down the private stairs to the Prime Minister's office. The guards outside the building had been doubled, and no one was allowed to enter or leave without a pass or in some instances, a complete search.

John A. Macdonald, Prime Minister of Canada, sat behind his desk. Passing his hand through a shock of graying hair, his deep-set eyes were pools of worry and fatigue. For days now, he had remained at his massive oak desk, reading reports from the North West, trying to sift the different advice given to him. Some advisors sneered at the Riel threat as being nothing more than the usual *métis* bragging. Others urged him to crush the *métis* without mercy.

Macdonald and his military aide, Colonel Carson, were smoking silently when another telegraph messenger knocked.

Macdonald took the message and said to Carson, "When will they stop coming? I wonder what this one says."

50 MEN BELIEVED FENIANS CROSSED WYO-
MING BORDER FAR WEST REGINA THIS WEEK
DIRECTION NORTH.

CROWDER

Colonel Carson, a lean-faced man in civilian clothes that did little to hide the fact he was a soldier, picked up a cup of cold coffee and drank it. He had been pacing, but now he sat down beside the P.M.'s desk.

"I don't think there's any doubt of the Fenians' coming in," he said. "Fifty isn't a large number, but there will be others. And they have what the *métis* don't have: money. Some of it is their own money, collected from the poor Irish in the back streets of New York and Boston and Chicago. The biggest part of it comes from American politicians, who are determined to annex this country. You have to act now, Prime Minister. There's no other way."

The Prime Minister nodded, still staring at the large wall map behind his desk. "We're a big country, Carson. That's one of our problems." He picked up a pointer and traced a line between Ottawa and Regina. He gave Regina a rap to express his annoyance.

"How," he said, "are we going to get troops from here to here without a lot of delays? Look at the distance involved. It frightens me."

"It doesn't have to, Prime Minister," Carson said calmly. "The troops can move west on the Canadian Pacific."

"But it isn't finished. You know that. They may never get it finished north of Lake Superior. Everything—track, locomotives—sinks in the muskeg. It's like trying to lay tract in quicksand. Van Horne has tried everything to beat that stretch and he still hasn't succeeded. That muskeg must be a thousand feet deep. Anyway, there are other unfinished stretches, too."

101

Carson said, "I took the liberty of asking Mr. Van Horne to come here tonight, sir."

"Why tonight?"

Carson smiled. "You have a way of making decisions on the third night, Prime Minister."

"Don't think you ever know me too well," John A. Macdonald cautioned. "But you're right. I had just about made up my mind to telegraph Middleton when Crowder's message came. The Fenians! If they want to fight England, they why the hell don't they go to England? You say Van Horne is coming?"

Carson looked at his watch. "He's been in the building for fifteen minutes. I was about to tell you."

"Then fetch him here, man. At once. Still, I have my doubts about sending a whole army by train. I don't think even the Americans have done that. By God, it would be something if we could do it!"

Colonel Carson went downstairs and came back in a few minutes with a barrel-shaped man in a hopsack suit and the look of one who hates to sit still for long. The Prime Minister came from behind his desk to greet him, for here was the greatest railroad builder in Canada, the United States, or anywhere else. Son of an old New York Dutch family, Van Horne believed there was nothing that couldn't be done if you tried hard enough. Van Horne was Canada's favorite American.

"Cigar?"

"Indeed, yes," Van Horne said, settling back in his chair.

"Whiskey?"

"Nothing goes better with a cigar."

They all had scotch whiskey.

"You are aware of what's happening in the North West, Mr. Van Horne?" the Prime Minister said. "Of course, you know some of it."

"Carson here has been filling me in," Van Horne said.

"And I get information from my own people in Saskatchewan. It has occurred to me that they may try to dynamite the tracks and cut the telegraph lines. I have had men patrolling the track for two weeks."

Macdonald said, "Then you do know how serious it is?"

"Not entirely, Prime Minister. But I know that any internal war, any civil war, must have terrible consequences. Look what happened to my own country. The effects will last for a long time. I would hate to see the same thing to take place here."

Macdonald said, "I'm told your motto is: 'If you want something done, name the day when it must be finished.'"

"Yes, I believe that." Van Horne smiled. "Give or take a day or two."

"Can you move five-thousand soldiers to Saskatchewan in a week? A week and a half at the latest?"

Van Horne regarded his smoldering cigar. "Yes, Prime Minister, I think a week to ten days would be all right. If we had a clear track, I could have them there in three days. But I'm not making excuses for the track. It will be finished before long."

"Are you sure, Mr. Van Horne?"

"As sure as I can be, Prime Minister. This isn't a snap judgment. I've been going over it since Colonel Carson first talked to me, and I have decided what can be done about the unfinished stretches of track. What's the final destination?"

"Fort Qu'Appelle."

Van Horne said, "It can be done, but it's going to be hell for the men. The worst part is the 105 miles of scattered gaps north of Lake Superior. You know that. Where I can, I will lay track on ice or snow and trust it to hold. There will be many places where that isn't possible. Some of the men will then travel by sleigh, but most will have to walk. We will have to leave trains behind when the tracks end. It will be easy for the men until we reach Lake Superior. Until that point, they can ride in regular passenger cars. On the far side of the lake, past the 105 miles of gaps, there are no passenger cars, just construction flatcards, with no sides, no roof, and no heat. But I can have my men working on those flatcars by morning, nailing up thick walls and looking for all the stoves they can find. Some of the men will travel comfortably enough; the others will be mighty cold. Some may die of it."

"It can't be helped."

Colonel Carson asked, "What about the artillery?"

"That's going to be the worst problem of all. If you didn't need it, I would say leave it behind. Yes, I know it has to go. But it's going to have to be loaded and unloaded a dozen times. There is nothing like trying to get a field piece on or off a flatcar when the temperature is fifty below. It gets that cold on the lake this time of year."

Macdonald didn't want to hear any more about hardship. "Do what has to be done, Mr. Van Horne. I will write you a letter of authorization right now. Colonel Carson will be your liaison between my office and the military. If anyone, and I don't care who he is or of what rank, refuses to cooperate or otherwise shows a disinclination to help, I will deal with him immediately."

Macdonald wrote as he talked, making broad angry strokes of the pen. He signed with a flourish and pressed a rubber stamp to the lower right-hand corner of the letter. "There," he said, passing the document across the desk.

Van Horne read it and said, "This makes me dictator of Canada for ten days!" He put the letter in his pocket and stood up. "I just want to ask you one thing more, Prime Minister. I anticipate trouble along the line when we get to Saskatchewan and have already taken precautions. But what about here?"

Macdonald said, "Most of our French-Canadian

citizens are loyal. There is talk of support for Riel and the *métis*, but," said Macdonald, smiling without much humor, "if you can deliver the troops to Fort Qu'Appelle on time, the talk around here will remain just talk."

Thirteen

The cold northern dawn was breaking when Sundance, Dumont, and fifty mounted *métis*, all seasoned frontiersman, saw Duck Lake up ahead through the whirling snow. The wind whipped through the pines, penetrating their thick wool clothing and fur-lined boots. Men and horses were blinded by snow as they plowed through the deepening drifts. Halfway between Batoche and Fort Carlton, the lake shone like silver in the weak half-light of the morning sun. Willows and poplars fringed the lake on all sides. On the far side of the lake were the log houses that contained the food, rifles, ammunition, and other supplies stored for use by the Mounties and the militia.

Wiping snow from his eyes, Dumont said, "It looks like we got here first, but we'd better make sure. One of my men in Fort Carlton said Superintendent Crozier was getting ready to seize the stores some time today."

"Makes sense," Sundance said. Dumont had just sent two men ahead to check for an ambush, and Sundance watched while their outlines became lost in the falling snow. Once they raided the supply camp, the *métis* would be in open rebellion against the government of Canada, as he would himself, Sundance knew. Before it was over, he might hang for it. So far, he hadn't come up with a plan that seemed to have any chance of working.

The two scouts rode back and reported that the camp was deserted. Dumont nodded. "So we win the first fight of this war. This is where it begins." The big *métis* shrugged. "Or where it ends."

They rode around the edge of the lake that was now beginning to thaw in the center. There were two log houses there, shuttered against the ice and wind. Both doors were secured with heavy padlocks. Dumont broke both locks with a hatchet, and they went in out of the cold. Rifles and boxes of ammunition took up most of the space in the first house; in the other, canned goods were stacked on shelves from floor to ceiling, with smoke-cured ham and frozen sides of beef hung from hooks. A rough table was piled high with blankets.

"We won't go hungry or cold, not for a while," Dumont said. "Those Lee-Metford bolt actions will make the Canadians wish they had let us go in peace."

Sundance picked up one of the fast-firing British-made military rifles. He tested the action; the short-pull bolt slid back and forth smoothly. "A fine gun," he agreed.

Dumont told his men to start loading the sleighs. "Don't overload. Take what you can, then throw the rest in the lake. We'll burn the houses before we move out."

The sleighs were about half loaded when a young *métis* on a winded horse came galloping from the other side of the lake. He jumped down, yelling, "Crozier and a big party of Mounties and militia are coming up fast. They have a seven-pound gun."

"How fast?" Dumont asked.

"Not much more than an hour, Gabriel. What are you going to do?"

"Ambush them," Dumont said calmly. "Have they spare horses?"

"All they need to catch up to us."

Dumont said, "Then we can't run, even if we wanted to. We can't trap them here, because Crozier might guess that's what we'll do. Let's ride out to greet the Canadians."

About a mile and a half from Duck Lake, Dumont found the position he wanted: a low hill intersecting the road, with ravines running forward on either side toward the police and militia and clumps of brush and willows to provide natural cover. He posted most of his men here while a smaller party occupied an abandoned cabin to the right of Superintendent Crozier's advance.

It was a perfect place for an ambush. Unaware of what lay in store for them, the police and militiamen trudged on through the falling snow. As the snow grew heavier, everything melded into the enveloping grayness. Crozier's men crossed the first ridge and started down into the valley. Then, half frozen, they climbed the next hill. Nothing moved yet in the snow-blotted distance. They were still climbing the icy slope when Crozier saw a line of *métis* riflemen in motion, snaking around his left flank.

As Crozier ordered his bewildered men to open fire, a deadly hail of bullets crackled from the *métis* line, ripping through the Canadian force with terrible effect. The *métis* were in deep cover while Crozier's men were out in the open, with not a rock or tree in sight. When the militia tried to expand their line, they came under intense fire from the abandoned cabin. Crozier ordered up the seven-pounder, but by then the militia had advanced too far and were in the line of fire.

Yelling like a madman, Crozier ordered the militia to fall back. The seven-pounder opened fire. After only three shots, an inexperienced gunner rammed in a shell before the powder, and the gun was put out of action. Rallied by Crozier, the militia made a direct assault on the cabin; however, they were driven back with heavy losses.

Mounting his horse, Gabriel Dumont ordered the

métis to counterattack. An instant later, his horse was shot out from under him and he fell heavily in the snow. The wound in his head opened again and he began to bleed. Sundance rushed to him and dragged him to his feet.

"Enough, Gabriel," he yelled above the crackle of rifle fire. "You've beaten them. Don't make it a slaughter. Let them retreat."

For a moment, Dumont fought to break Sundance's hold on him. Blood dripped from his head, staining his dark blue coat. The fury died in his eyes and he started to sag. Down the slope, the *métis* were driving the Canadians force back into the blinding snow. Dead Mounties and militiamen lay everywhere. Then, after a few more outbursts of firing, the fight was over. It had been a decisive victory for the *métis*; they had even captured the seven-pound cannon.

"The funny thing is, I don't hate them," Dumont said, watching while the *métis* collected weapons from the dead Mounties. "They are hard men, but they have always been fair according to their rules, their law. They are nothing like your United States cavalry. But the militia are volunteers, and they would like to destroy us, drive us from our land and far into the icy regions. Before they do that, we will give them a fight to remember."

Sundance said, "Then you don't think you're going to win?"

Dumont rubbed his snow-crusted beard and looked very tired. He raised his rifle when he saw one of his men going through a dead policeman's pocket. He fired one shot and the looter jumped back in terror.

"Only the guns, Henri," he roared. "Take anything else, and I'll shoot your eyes out."

Turning back to Sundance, he said quietly, "You ask are we going to win. You have served with the Americans, and you know that the white men are like locusts. Kill a hundred, and soon you are faced with a thousand more. Do *you* think we're going to win?"

Sundance liked the big, life-hardened buffalo hunter. He spoke the truth. "No, my friend, but maybe you can make it so costly for them that they'll come to some kind of terms. I think that's the best you can hope for. You can't win big battles against them. Let them see what you can do, then give them a chance to think about it. My advice is: Don't push them to the point where they can't back off."

"I think that is good advice," Dumont agreed, looking at Sundance with narrowed eyes. "We will strike at the other towns and forts along the Saskatchewan and we will take them. Then, when we are in a position of strength, a good place to bargain from, we will send them our terms. If they refuse to bargain, we will fight on until we are all dead. But killing us all will not be easy. Before they have done it, we will make the name of Canada stink in the nostrils of the world."

Dumont waved his hand toward the bleak landscape, made even more bleak by the corpses dotting the slope. "This is our land, this wilderness that nobody wanted until they smelled the money to be made here. Our ancestors are buried here in the frozen earth. We were here before there were maps, and we will die here if we have to."

There was nothing to be said, Sundance knew, because in his bones he felt the love these brave people had for their windswept land. He knew the bitterness they felt at being cornered, fenced off by laws that meant nothing to them. The law—white man's law—had no meaning for the halfbreed or the Indian. The land itself was all that mattered. In their way, the whites loved the land, too, but to them it was always property, something to be coveted and fought over, not something to be felt in the blood and bones.

Turning his horse away from the battlefield, Dumont said, "I owe you my life, Sundance, so I will say this now—it is not too late for you to get out."

"No," Sundance answered. "I'm here, and here I stay."

Fourteen

On the night of March 28, 1885, Sundance, Dumont, and Riel, accompanied by a large force of well-armed *métis*, watched the evacuation of Fort Carlton by the Mounties and militia. From a long, sloping ridge they listened to the shouts of command as the Canadians moved out, led by Commissioner Irvine.

The day before, after learning of the defeat at Duck Lake, Irvine had decided there was no choice but to abandon the fort. The old fur trader's post had not been built for defense. It was on the river's edge, and the three-hundred foot hill behind it commanded the fort square from all sides. In addition, the militiamen, all drawn from Fort Albert, wanted to get back to their families, now undefended.

"We could strike now," Dumont said. "They are already in a rout."

Riel said, "No. We will save our strength for the bigger battles ahead. The Indians will soon be joining us. Already I have sent news of Duck Lake. All they need is a little more persuasion. Soon, all the towns on the Saskatchewan will be in our hands. But listen to me, Gabriel. The Irishman is growing impatient. He wanted to be with us tonight. Hardesty and his Irishmen have come a long way to fight on our side."

Dumont said, "Let him stay in Batoche and wait for the rest of his men to come from the States. We will use them when the time comes. There will be plenty of fighting for Hardesty before this war is over."

Riel said, "I think you would like to win this war without his help. Speak plainly, old friend. Is that what you're thinking?"

"It would be better if we could. If we can't, well, so be it."

Turning to Sundance, Riel said, "You have become Gabriel's friend. He trusts your judgment. What is your opinion?"

Sundance said, "So far, the fight has been between you and the Canadians. Turning foreigners, paid mercenaries, against them will make them angrier than they are now. No country likes to be invaded by foreigners. Even the French-Canadians in the east may turn against you. I would say keep the Irish out of the fighting if you don't need them."

Riel sighed. "You are probably right, but it's so hard to decide. Everything keeps changing from day to day. What I don't understand, Gabriel, is why you have changed your mind. Two weeks ago you were ready to welcome the Irishman."

"Two weeks ago I hadn't met Hardesty. There is something about the man I don't like and don't trust. I have been thinking that, if we win this war, Hardesty and his band of trained soldiers won't be so easy to get rid of. Hardesty talks of bringing in a thousand men, maybe more. Most of these men have no families to care about, and I think many are criminals and killers."

Riel said, "Say what you have to say, Gabriel. There is more."

"Already there is bad feeling between these Irishmen

and our men. Our women . . ." Dumont spat in the snow. "Hardesty is too eager to set the Indians against the whites. He would bathe the country in blood from here to the Rockies. Who can say what mad plan he has? To seize the whole North West and hold it with American support."

"This is incredible," Riel said. "Hardesty has accepted my leadership without question."

Sundance said, "Not so incredible. Other bold men have tried to build their own empires. Walker tried it in Nicaragua and nearly succeeded. He ended up in front of a firing squad, but he gave it a fair try."

Riel's voice faltered a little. "I would not permit such a thing. I have given my word to my people."

Dumont spat again. Sundance didn't say anything.

"They're moving out," Dumont said. "The fort is on fire."

Flames streaked the night sky as the last of the garrison disappeared into the darkness, taking the road along the edge of the river. Horsemen led the way, followed by sleighs, while more mounted men brought up the rear. Then the last sounds died away and there was nothing but the fretting of the horses and the ever-present wind blowing from the north.

"I wish they'd all go as quietly as that," Riel said, clapping his mittened hands together. The *métis* leader was a man of constantly changing moods. Now he was cheerful again, all talk of Hardesty forgotten. "Maybe they will, my friends. They are just men, like us, and do not wish to die. We can live in peace with the Canadians, the English Canadians. If only they could realize that we are not a subject people. Come on now. Let us look at what is left of Fort Carlton."

There wasn't much left by the time they reached the burning buildings. The Canadians had left nothing that could be salvaged. The flag had been lowered and taken away; the flagpole stood gaunt against the glare of the flames.

"Chop it down," Dumont ordered. "Chop it down and burn it."

The *métis* cheered as the flagpole toppled to the ground. Scouts were sent out to watch for a counterattack by Irvine's forces, while cook fires were started and the pungent smell of thick pea soup with chunks of ham rose into the frosty night air. It stopped snowing and the wind died down. Around the fire, they ate with the appetites of men who had been long on the trail. The buildings of the fort were all but gone.

Hunkered down beside the fire, Dumont sniffed the air. "The spring will be here earlier than we thought. I can smell the thaw coming. We must move on Fort Battleford without delay. Winter is our friend and we must make use of it while we can. Already the people from the town have moved into the fort. It is well fortified, and taking it will not be like Duck Lake or this place here. They know we are coming and will be waiting. Our men will die in the taking of the fort, but there isn't time to starve them out."

"What about Fort Pitt?" Riel asked. "There is a garrison there."

"It is not so important as Battleford, Louis. After taking Battleford, we can pass it by, then attack Fort Albert. Pitt will be caught in the middle, with our forces to the north and south of it. Are you sure the Indians will be at war by the time we reach Battleford?"

"I am sure, Gabriel. Dumas has gone ahead to the reservation. If any man can rouse the Indians, Dumas can. He says Little Bear and Poundmaker can throw nine-hundred braves against the Canadians, more than that if other tribes join the war. For years, Poundmaker's people have starved on the Battleford reservation—bad food, what there is of it, not enough blankets to keep the women and children from freezing. Yes, Gabriel,

Poundmaker and his people have had enough of Canadian promises. They will fight."

Sundance asked, "But can they be stopped once the killing starts?"

Riel's deep voice was still full of confidence. "Any man is only as good as he is treated. Give the Crees and the Stoneys food and blankets, give them back their pride as men, and they will see us only as friends. They will stop because I tell them to stop."

Dumont had no comment to make, and it wasn't because of the chunk of steaming ham he had just put in his mouth. He looked from Riel to Sundance, then began to scrape out his plate. He stood up and wiped snow from the barrel of his Lee-Medford repeater.

"It is time to go," he said, "if we want to get there by first light."

It snowed lightly during the night, but the sun was trying to break through by the time they reached the outskirts of Battleford. Long before they got there they heard the sound of rifle fire. At first it was uneven, but it grew more concentrated as the sun broke through the watery sky. They topped a ridge, and from the summit they could see down into the valley containing the town and the fort.

Dumont took a short brass telescope from his pocket and opened it and grunted with satisfaction at what he saw. Riel took the telescope and scanned the valley.

"It looks like Dumas did his work all right," Dumont said. "The town is deserted except for Dumas and the Indians. Everybody else is in the fort."

Riel handed the telescope to Sundance. He moved it from the town to the fort, some distance away, and back again. Most of the firing was being done by the Indians, now under cover of the houses closest to the stockade. The Indians were all in war paint. While Sundance watched, a group of them tried to rush the main gate, only to be driven back with the loss of half their number.

Dumont cursed. "What does Dumas think he's doing? His orders were to pin them down in the fort, not to get half the Indians killed."

"You should have taken the Gatling gun from Batoche," Riel said. "It would make all the difference now."

"No, Louis, Batoche is the center of our country, our capital. It must be defended by every means. If Batoche fell, it would take the heart out of our people."

The fort was on a hillside some distance from the town. The Indians had already ridden up to parley. By that time, they had plundered the stores and buildings of the town. Inside the fort there were six-hundred settlers and townspeople, three hundred of them women and children. They watched fearfully through rifle slits while the Indians dressed themselves in silk party gowns and bonnets, screaming like maniacs while they guzzled whiskey and hacked pianos to bits with their tomahawks.

When the attempt at holding a parlay failed, the Indians fell back before they attacked. Driven back by rifle fire from the stockade, they waved a flag of truce before encircling the fort, waiting for it to surrender. Now they were attacking again.

Followed by Sundance and Riel, Dumont galloped down the slope toward the town, yelling at the Indians to fall back. He jumped off his horse and grabbed one of the *métis* who was with the Indians.

"Where is Dumas?" he roared, trying to make himself heard above the war crys of the Indians.

"Dead! Shot!" the man yelled back. "The Indians will no longer obey their leaders."

"They will obey me," Dumont roared. Taking no heed of the bullets from the fort, he rode his horse straight into a bunch of Indians who were fighting over a bottle of whiskey. One Indian swung a tomahawk at Dumont.

Dumont upended his rifle and struck the brave between the eyes with the brass-shod butt. The Indian grunted and went down. Another whiskey-crazed brave jumped at Dumont with a knife. Dumont jerked his foot from the stirrup and kicked him squarely in the face. Then Dumont rounded his horse and knocked the others sprawling in the snow.

"Get back!" Dumont yelled. "Get back under cover."

"What do you think?" Sundance asked Dumont when they were crouched down inside the broken window of a thick-walled cabin. Now that the Indians had pulled back, the fire from the fort had slackened. Riel had gone to talk to the Indian chiefs, followed by the *métis* Dumont had appointed in Dumas's place.

"Do you think that seven-inch cannon can be put in working order?" Dumont asked. "If it can't, I have been thinking about fire arrows."

"There are hundreds of women and children in there. You want to burn them out?"

"I want to capture that fort. We can't leave a garrison behind us. What about the cannon?"

"The shell can be pried out," Sundance answered. "It will take time, but it can be done. We only have two shells and just enough powder to fire them. The militia managed to save the rest when they retreated at Duck Lake. But for all they know in the fort, we could have all the shot and powder we need."

Dumont asked, "Can you do it, get the gun back in working order?"

"I've seen it done. You heat the barrel very fast over a fire. The shell isn't explosive, it's just a ball propelled by powder. If there is no powder in the barrel, there's no danger of an explosion. The barrel heats faster than the ball and expands faster. Then you hoist the gun with ropes, muzzle pointing straight down, and hit the breech hard with a sledgehammer or something else. With luck, and if it isn't too badly jammed, the ball will fall out. Then you let the barrel cool slowly so there won't be any distortion."

Dumont ordered his men to bring the cannon up from the rear of his column. Sundance found the town's one blacksmith shop and ordered the seven-pounder brought there. He pumped the bellows and got the fire in the forge white hot again. "Get the chains on the gun," he ordered. "Don't bring it down too close to the fire. I'll tell you how close. Once it starts to get hot, keep the barrel turning. Do it at a steady pace. It has to heat evenly. Once it's hot, don't let it drop or bang into something. If the barrel gets bent, there is no way we can straighten it. All right now, start lowering it toward the fire. Easy, not so fast. I'll tell you when it's hot enough, then point the muzzle toward the ground and make sure it doesn't swing when I start hitting it with the sledge."

Dumont and Sundance watched closely while the barrel of the cannon was rotated above the flame. Soon it began to glow a dull red; before long the red turned to white.

"Quickly now," Sundance said. "Point the muzzle downward and hold it firm. Move before the ball expands as much as the barrel."

Sundance had pulled a keg close to the forge. Now he climbed up on it, measuring for the first swing of the sledge. If it took more than two or three blows, it wouldn't work. He wanted it to work; he wanted the garrison in the fort to surrender.

Lifting the heavy sledge-hammer and sweating in the fierce glow of the fire, he struck the back of the cannon. The three *métis* held it firmly under the impact of the blow. Sundance raised the sledge-hammer again and struck the gun in the same place. Inside the gun there seemed to be a small shifting movement. Without waiting, Sundance put all his weight behind the third blow. With it, the *métis* yelled as the ball rattled out of the barrel and fell on the floor.

"Let the cannon hang the way it is, muzzle straight down," Sundance said. "And keep that door closed so it won't cool too fast."

They waited for the barrel of the seven-pounder to cool. Doing it carefully took more than half an hour. Sundance ordered the *métis* to put the gun back on its carriage and he ran his hand over the still-warm barrel. "It looks all right. We'll know for sure as soon as I fire it."

Dumont grinned. "You mean it will blow up if it isn't all right?"

"I'd say so."

"Then I'll fire it."

"No, I fixed it—at least, I hope I did—so I'll touch it off. But first I'd like you to get Louis and have him talk to the commander of the garrison. They may be willing to surrender to you but not to the Indians. If they're afraid enough of the Indians, especially the Crees, they would rather die fighting than be scalped and tortured. Louis has to give his word that the Indians won't harm them, that they are free to march into Alberta with a safe conduct all the way. If Louis allows the Indians to massacre them, it could well be the end of your cause. There would be no bargaining with the Canadians if that happened."

Dumont nodded. "I will go and find him. Where will you be when I am doing that?"

"Pointing the seven-pounder straight at the gate of the fort. It may take one shell to get them to parlay. But in the end, it's up to Louis and how convincing he can be. I'd hate to see them make a real fight of it."

Sundance positioned the cannon between two log houses after pushing a wagon out in front of the gun. Under cover of the wagon, he primed the gun, then rammed in the ball. He lined up the muzzle with the gate, then adjusted it for the drop of the shell. If he hadn't misjudged, the shell would strike the log gate about halfway to the top, just where the crossbar would be on the inside. One shell might not smash open the gate; maybe even two wouldn't be enough. What was going to happen next depended on so many things.

Dumont came back with Riel, who was carrying a flag of truce, a white tablecloth tied to a broomstick. Poundmaker, chief of the Crees, was with them. At first, Riel wanted to walk right out in the open waving his peace flag. Dumont and Sundance had to hold him back.

Riel didn't seem to understand, "But they wouldn't shoot me. I am not armed. I carry a flag of truce."

"Wait," Sundance warned him. "Somebody might shoot you. It doesn't have to be a Mountie, but one of the militiamen might take a crack at you."

"Then what do you propose to do, Sundance?" Riel gripped his broomstick with fierce determination.

"Fire a shot at the gate. One shot to show them what we can do if they refuse to surrender. They have no way of knowing that we only have two shells. After that, you can talk. They will want to be very sure about the Indians. Otherwise, we're in for a long fight."

"Cover me," Sundance said to Dumont. "Tell the *métis* to fire over the heads of the men on the stockade."

Dumont rapped out the order. Immediately, a hail of lead was thrown at the fort, the *métis* firing the ten-round Lee-Metfords as fast as they could work the bolts.

Sundance and Dumont manhandled the cannon around the side of the wagon. "Get back now," Sundance warned Dumont. "Your people need you more than they need me." He adjusted the range and elevation again. It looked all right, as good as he could make it. A lot of lives were riding on those two shells.

"Now!"

He touched a lighted fuse to the cannon. It dug back on its wooden carriage as the shell screamed straight at the gate of the fort, going slightly higher than he had figured. There was a splintering crash as some of the thick verticals in the gate gave way. White smoke boiled up from the muzzle of the cannon, and from the *métis* ranks a wild cheer went up.

Sundance took the peace flag from Riel's hand and waved it from behind the wagon. A flurry of shots came its way. He yelled and waved the flag again. This time there was only one shot, then a man's voice on the stockade yelling for the defenders to cease firing.

"What do you want out there?" the same voice called out.

"To talk," Sundance answered. "We demand your surrender and will guarantee safe passage to Alberta. Louis Riel is here and wants to talk to you. He will walk out under a flag of truce. If anybody shoots at him, you will all be killed. No one will be spared. Do I have your word?"

"Who are you?"

"My name is Jim Sundance. And yours?"

"Inspector Kennedy, Royal North West Mounted Police. You have my word. Riel will not be shot. I am coming out now with one of my men. You will walk with Riel?"

Sundance said he would. He took the flag of truce from Riel and began to walk toward the gate. Dumont and the *métis* watched from cover, their fingers twitching on the triggers of their rifles.

Riel and Sundance walked without hurry, the crunching of their boots in the muddy snow being the only sound heard on the slope that went up to the gate. Then the gate opened and a tall Mountie officer with bushy red hair came out followed by a noncommissioned police-man. Both men had left their sidearms behind. The gate closed. They met about twenty-five yards from the gate.

Kennedy, the officer, looked from Riel to Sundance

with frosty blue eyes. He was about thirty and stood very straight. His fair skin was reddened by the cold. "Do you have any idea of what you're doing?" he rasped in a British military voice. It was a voice well accustomed to being obeyed instantly. He was speaking to Riel. "You are in armed rebellion against the Dominion of Canada. Do you know what that means? Do you realize what you're facing? I advise you to put down your arms immediately. Of course, you realize I can promise you nothing but a fair trial. Well, what do you have to say for yourselves?"

Sundance couldn't help grinning at the arrogant Britisher. "I can promise you something better than that," he said. "Unless you surrender and march out of here, we will blow the fort to bits, then burn it."

Fifteen

Major General Frederick Middleton's beefy face was almost as red as the tunic he wore. Usually, it was red from many years of drinking brandy and soda in the far corners of the British Empire. A veteran of the Indian Mutiny and the savage Maori Wars of New Zealand, General Middleton was an Englishman and never let anyone forget it for a minute, especially the Canadians he was now forced to command.

On this bright morning in April 1885, the General's face was red as with rage, not brandy. After a lifetime of service to the Empire, the bad-tempered old soldier had been sent from England to take command of all the Canadian militia, in all the provinces and territories. It was not a job that appealed to him, but it was either that or face compulsory retirement. The old warhorse had been put out to pasture in Canada in a post that was supposed to be a sinecure. By the time he had arrived in the Dominion, he had become paunchy, stodgy, opinion-ated, and openly contemptuous of the fighting abilities of the Canadian militia. Now he had a rebellion on his hands.

Waving the telegraph message he had just received

from Prime Minister John Macdonald, the General sputtered with anger while his aide, Captain Winfield, another Englishman, listened in sympathy. General Middleton trusted no one but the British officers or former British officers on his staff.

"Damn these colonials!" Middleton was raging. "Who the blazes is this fellow Riel? I never heard of him before this week. Who in hell is he, and what does he want?"

"Riel is leader of the *métis*, sir. That's what the halfbreeds are called. Riel wants to establish a separate country."

"Yes! Yes! I've been told all that. They tell me he's even tried it before. Why didn't they hang him the first time, when they had the chance? A length of strong hemp would have settled the whole blasted problem. Now I'm supposed to go up there and clean up this mess. And what have I got to do it with? A thousand ragtag militiamen who hardly know one end of a rifle from the other. Probably half of them are in sympathy with this mongrel Riel. Ah, Winfield, if only I had two-hundred British regulars, I'd march up the Saskatchewan, burn their towns and hand the ringleaders. I'd give them a trial all right, about thirty seconds of a trial, then . . ."

General Middleton twisted his thick neck to one side and made a strangling sound. "By God, I gave those buggers what for in India. I'd like to do the same here. Burn them out. That's all these savages understand. Burn them out and hang a few dozen for good measure."

Captain Winfield said without irony, "So far, sir, the *métis* have been doing most of the burning. Fort Carlton and Fort Battleford have already been burned to the ground. However, except for the battle at Duck Lake, there has been remarkably little bloodshed. Even the Indians seem to be under some kind of control."

General Middleton scowled as he hacked at his breakfast of bacon, liver sausage, and eggs. "If I had my regulars, I'd put them under control all right. I can't say I have much respect for the Americans, but they do seem to know how to deal with savages. Treat them kindly and they think you're stupid. The iron fist, hot lead, cold steel—that's what they respect. They look up to the man who can flog them back into place."

"Do you have a plan of battle, sir?" Winfield drank the tea the General had graciously poured for him.

Behind the General, there was a map of the North West Territories on the wall. He picked up a ruler from the table and tapped Fort Qu'Appelle. "That's where we are, and up there is Batoche. That is where we will strike, at the heart of this miserable rebellion. That is where their women and children are concentrated. Once we take Batoche, the back of this rebellion will be broken."

Wingate asked, "When you say strike, did you mean cavalry, sir?"

"I do not! This isn't country for cavalry. No, Winfield, we will do it the way the British army has always done in its wars. The old foot-slogging infantryman may not have the dash of the cavalry, but he gets the job done. Let these halfbreeds gallop about on their ponies as much as they like. While they are doing it, we will march into the heart of their country. Of course, we will use the militia cavalry, but only to guard our communications. Always watch your communications, Winfield, because if you don't, some fine day you'll find yourself cut off, isolated. A lifetime of campaigning has taught me that."

"What about the two other forces, sir? General Strange's and Colonel Otter's. General Strange is on his way to Edmonton with six-hundred men. Colonel Otter is moving north with another six hundred. Here in Fort Qu'Appelle we have eight-hundred men, including the Winnipeg and Ontario cavalry. Colonel Dennison thinks we should send a strong force of cavalry to drive the métis out of the towns they have taken. By the time they can regroup, our main force will command the whole Saskatchewan Valley."

At the mention of Dennison's name, the General's face grew even redder. "Dennison would like to make a name for himself, become the General Custer of the North West. Well, sir, we all know what happened to him. The Winnipeg and Ontario cavalry will guard our supply depots. There isn't much glory in that, but the Colonel will have to make the best of it."

"The Prime Minister requests an answer to his message, sir," Winfield said as diplomatically as he could. "His suggestion was that you move at once. What do you want me to say, sir?"

"Tell that gibbering Scottish idiot to go to the hottest part of hell. And while you're at it, ask him how many wars he fought in. Ask him if he ever did anything in his life besides sucking around for votes."

Winfield waited patiently.

General Middleton raged on. Finally, he said, "Tell Macdonald I'll move as soon as I'm ready. If that doesn't suit him, tell him to take it up with Her Majesty's government. No, don't say that. Just say I'll move when ready. But do tell them this. Request that the five-hundred British regulars now stationed in Nova Scotia be sent here immediately."

Winfield finished writing the message. "Mr. Macdonald may not like that, sir. He's already told the newspapers that he is determined to keep the Dominion intact at all costs. He speaks of an all-Canadian army. I think he sees himself as another Abraham Lincoln."

Middleton stabbed at an egg and let the yolk run out. "Macdonald's a bloody fool, but I still request transfer of the British regulars. I don't care how many Canadian militiamen are being sent from the east. I want those regulars if I can get them. Then you'll see those half-castes run. I don't think Macdonald will grant my request. What

127

I want is to get it down in writing."

General Middleton finished his tea and sat back in his chair. Winfield hurried to light his cigar. "Thanks, my boy," the General said, his anger fading away as he thought of the campaign ahead. "In a way, it's going to be good to get out from behind a desk and into the field. It isn't much of a war, but it's the only one we've got, I suppose. But what a country to fight it in! These half-caste blighters—what did you say they're called?"

"They call themselves the *métis*. I think it means, the people."

"The people, eh! Peculiar thing to call themselves. I wonder. Can they fight, do you think? Not just burn a few isolated posts, but really fight. The Maoris in New Zealand fought like tigers. And during the Mutiny, the sepoys were a pretty game lot. But these half-castes are quite new, quite strange to me. I suppose they're strange to everyone."

Winfield's voice was quiet. "From what I've been told, they fight very well. They believe they have nothing much to lose."

"Their lives, of course. Oh, I see what you mean. Well, that's going to make this campaign all the more interesting. Isn't it?"

"A campaign to be remembered, sir," Captain Winfield said.

After Inspector Kennedy had surrendered the fort and marched away with his people, Gabriel Dumont ordered the stockade burned. "But do not burn the town," he warned his men. "If the people who lived there want to return when the war is over, they are free to do so. Everything must be left as it is. We will have no use for the fort."

Riel was sitting on a waterproof blanket in the snow. He looked at the burning fort and sighed with satisfaction. "These have been fine victories, my friends. It seems as if God is with us. They run from us like sheep, even the Mounties. Do you remember, Gabriel, when the Mounties were first established? Ten or twelve years ago it was. One Mountie was worth a hundred men, white or red or halfbreed. Kill a Mountie, they said, and you would be hunted to the ends of the earth."

Sundance looked up from his food as Riel laughed harshly. There was no way to know how to take this man. One moment he was the commonsense and gentle leader of his downtrodden people; the next he was gloating over the number of men they had killed.

"We have killed many Mounties," Riel said, "and we are not hunted. Instead, we are the hunters. The Mounties died by the dozen at Duck Lake, and they slunk away from Fort Carlton and Fort Pitt like whipped dogs. And they talk of the power of that pudgy old woman they call the Great White Mother. The Great White Mother will take care of you, they told the Indians."

Riel laughed again. "The Great White Mother cannot even take care of them."

"They would have fought if the women and children hadn't been there," Dumont said. "Do not count on them always running."

"I did not know you admired the Redcoats so much, Gabriel."

"I admire all brave men, Louis. It is best to know the kind of men we face. When the women and children of the settlers and militia have been cleared from the Saskatchewan Valley, there will be fighting. It won't be like the fighting that has been going on. I think, when we have taken Fort Pitt, we should offer to make peace on our terms."

Staring into the fire, Riel said, "Is that what you think, Gabriel? You think they will want to make peace? But there is another question, one even more important, and that is: Do we want to make peace so soon? Is it not possible that *we* do not have to come to terms? What if our terms are simply get your forces out of Saskatchewan and do not return?"

Sundance knew it wasn't his place to interfere in this discussion. He knew, too, that arguing with Riel when he was in a certain mood was a waste of time.

"You are so silent, Gabriel," Riel said. "Why is that?"

"Because I am thinking what it would be like to have peace again along the Saskatchewan. Very soon there will be spring flowers on the prairie and along the banks of the river. The sun will be warm and the days long and the wind from the north not so cold. I would like to see peace before the end of spring."

Riel said, "It may not come by next spring. Who can say when it will come? Perhaps it will never come for the *métis*. We must accept the inevitable."

"Nothing is inevitable, Louis."

"For some men it is, my friend. It may be that way for me. Often, late at night when I can't sleep, I think it is. Some things can't be changed."

"Nothing is inevitable," Dumont said.

"Perhaps not for you. You are a good man, but there are some things you don't understand."

"I understand that I am going to blow the railroad bridges on the Canadian Pacific. More than five-thousand men are on their way from the east by rail. I don't know where they are now, but I would think more than half way. That is why some of us have to ride south and do what we can to tear up the tracks. But the bridges and tunnels are more important than the tracks."

"But you are needed here, Gabriel. I am no general."

Dumont said, "I will send Boudreau and Roberge. They will take twenty men. I know the tunnels and bridges will be heavily guarded, but we have to hope. If we can stop the main force long enough, we can deal with the others. They are not so many, and the old Englishman who leads them, Middleton, is slow and cautious."

While they were talking, a rider came into camp at full gallop. "It's one of the relay men," Dumont said. They all stood up. Sundance had already guessed what it was.

"They're on the move," the relay rider said. "Middleton and a thousand men left Fort Qu'Appelle the day before yesterday. They have a big supply train guarded by cavalry, with Gatling guns and cannon."

Dumont looked puzzled. "The cavalry is guarding the rear? I do not understand. Are you sure of what you're saying? Have any cavalry units been sent forward of the column?"

"No. Our scouts have been watching them ever since they left the fort."

"What about scouts?"

"There are some scouts." The relay rider smiled. "But they do not scout so well. Or maybe they are acting under stupid orders. The whole column is moving very slowly."

"Good! The slower they move, the more time we have to get ready for them. Any news from the east and west? They will come at us from three sides. Anything from the north?"

"Not yet, Gabriel."

"All right, get something to eat, then ride back. Tell Campeau to send extra men to watch east and west. General Strange commands in Alberta, and he will come from there. But the man we have to worry about is General Otter from the east."

"Why Otter?" Sundance asked after the relay rider left.

"A Canadian," Dumont answered. "His is a rich lawyer who has written books on war. Twenty years ago, as a very young man, he served with your General Sheridan's cavalry. Ever since then he has been arguing, in Parliament and out, that cavalry is the driving force of a modern army. Of course, he is right, though the old men in Ottawa don't agree with him. I would say that, right now, General Otter is delighted to have this opportunity to prove how right his arguments are. That is why I think we have more to fear from him than from Middleton's main force. True, Otter is a militia officer and not a regular. It makes no difference. As a soldier, he is worth more than ten stupid Englishmen."

Sundance said, "If he rode with Sheridan, then he believes in the fire and the sword. Does he?"

"I have been thinking about that," Dumont answered. "If he starts to kill our people and burn our farms, we will answer him in kind. I pray he does not. But if he does, then we will show them what the word 'savage' means."

Dumont smiled bitterly. "They call us savages. I hope they don't make us prove it. We have spared many lives since this fight began. If they start killing, we will spare no more. One thing you can be sure of with Otter, and that is he won't worry much about supply lines. He'll carry all the supplies he can and forage for the rest. He once wrote that every cavalry unit ought to take along extra horses, not to be ridden but to be eaten when the food ran out."

"Sounds like a smart soldier," was Sundance's only comment.

Later, after Riel had wrapped himself in a buffalo robe and was sleeping close to the fire, Sundance and Dumont talked.

"He is marching on Batoche. Of that I am sure," Dumont said. "That is what I would do. I cannot let him take it. We could retreat to the north and draw his force in after us, then strike him in a number of suprise attacks." Dumont shook his head. "That would be the military way to do it, but I can't. Batoche must not fall."

"Then maybe now is the time to try to come to terms. It looks like this general, Middleton, isn't that eager to fight."

"I don't think he will come to terms, not yet. We must show him what it's going to mean to Canada if the fighting goes on. Anyway, Middleton has no authority to make a bargain with us. That will be up to Macdonald. It would be easier if some other man ruled in Ottawa."

"Why? Does Macdonald hate the *métis*?"

Dumont lowered his voice. "Not the *métis*. Louis Riel. He could have hanged Louis after the first rebellion, but he let him go to Montana instead. Maybe some of it was mercy. Most of it, I think, was politics. To have hanged Louis would have turned the French-Canadians against Macdonald's government. But no matter, Macdonald let Louis go free and suffered much abuse because of it. Ontario turned against him, wanted to kick him out. There was an unspoken agreement between Macdonald and Louis: his life in exchange for permanent exile in the United States. From where Macdonald sits, Louis broke his word. I suppose he did."

Sundance said, "Then it won't be easy no matter what happens."

"That's right. Macdonald can't back down again, even if he wants to. It would make him look like a fool, and no man wants to look like a fool. But Louis is our leader. He has kept our cause alive all these years, and we must follow him wherever it takes us. Now I think we'd better get some sleep. Dawn comes quickly, and there is much to be done. Soon we will discover what it is like to fight a real English general."

"You don't like the English, do you?"

"Not much."

"My father was an Englishman."

"I think he was a different kind of Englishman."

They both laughed.

Sixteen

Every step of Middleton's advance was being watched by *métis* scouts. There was even a *métis* spy working as a freighthandler in Middleton's wagon train. The column moved as ponderously as the mind of its commander. To the rear, the cavalry officers cursed the inactivity, the slow pace, the futility of not being able to take action. It began to snow again, though it wasn't as cold as it had been. Under a slate-colored sky, the combined force plodded on.

General Middleton, it seemed, was in no hurry to engage the enemy. His tent was elaborate and had a wooden floor made in sections, a folding bed piled with blankets, and buffalo robes. He had even brought along books and a chess set. At night, a small brazier of charcoal heated his quilted tent. He ate well, drank well, and slept well. There were many meetings with the staff of English officers. When it became necessary to have some of the Canadian militia officers present, he invariably disregarded their suggestions with a grunt or a growl.

The General liked to look at maps. The more maps the better. He used his ruler to measure distances, not knowing that, often, the shortest distance between two points was right through the middle of a swamp. Captain Winfield, the ambitious young career officer, was still his favorite audience. Middleton's meals were as elaborate as the rest of his equipment. Winfield was always glad to dine with the General because the food was so good: steak, glazed ham, fresh bread, baked potatoes. And always brandy and fine cigars.

General Middleton would say, "War is a science if nothing else. Strategy is what counts. Consider the situation carefully, then act on it. But always be sure of what you're doing. I have been a soldier more years than you are old, my boy, and I always know exactly how to proceed. Only fools rush in. Always remember that. I don't want to sound boastful, but I didn't get to be a major general in the best army in the world for nothing."

The General paused and Winfield came in quickly with, "You've had a most distinguished career, sir. Would you like to continue dictating your memoirs tonight?"

While the *métis* scouts watched silent and unseen, General Middleton, mellow with good food and aged brandy, would lie on his comfortable bed, with the charcoal brazier throwing off steady heat, and talk on and on about the campaigns of thirty years before.

"During the Indian mutiny, a regrettable episode in our history, we were forced to take stern measures against the ringleaders. One particularly severe form of execution was to tie a man across the mouth of a cannon."

Middleton's scouts reported back that there was no sign of the enemy. But the moment the scouts had ridden past, the *métis* would emerge from their hiding places. The snow stopped and the weather was bright and clear for a while. The column, slow as it was, was getting closer to Batoche. Soon it was only twenty-two miles away.

"If he doesn't drink too much, then it must be old age," Gabriel Dumont remarked to Sundance. Our man in the column reports that he sits up half the night in his tent, reading and playing chess. His breakfast takes an hour. There have been times when my scouts were close enough to shoot him through the head. When I heard that one of them almost did, I sent word that not a hair on his thick head must be touched."

Dumont began to laugh and Sundance had to grin. "Middleton is our friend. I love him like a brother," Dumont said. "Oh, please God, let him continue the way he is going. I know! I know! Sometimes wars are won by fools. It is time to stop him *now*!"

Middleton's right column of about five-hundred men was in camp about twenty miles south of Batoche. His left column, with the same number of men, was on the other side of the river.

Seventeen miles south of Batoche, on the east side of the South Satkatchewan River, Fish Creek emptied into the broad river and cut a forty-foot-deep ravine across the prairie. It was on all the maps, but General Middleton didn't seem to have given it any thought.

"This is where we will surprise them," Gabriel Dumont decided. There, part way down the slope nearest the Canadian advance, he posted one-hundred and fifty of his men. He led another fifty mounted *métis* further south to hide them in a coulee so that they could swoop down on the Canadian rear and herd them into the trap.

"It should work," Sundance agreed.

Early on April 24th, Middleton broke camp and moved forward, his scouts out in front. Then, for the first time, the scouts earned their keep. Riding back fast, they reported finding horse tracks on the road. The alarm was sounded, and Dumont's fifty horseman had to make a hasty retreat to the deep ravine. For once, Dumont's cunning had failed—and the fight was on.

In the ravine, the *métis* had dug rifle pits. If Middleton were a more intelligent commander, he would not have sent his force directly against the ravine. But that was what he did. On and on the Canadians came. When they reached the edge of the ravine, the *métis* opened fire, driving them back with heavy losses.

Middleton ordered his two cannons to open fire, but no damage was done to the concealed *métis*. Desperate now, he sent a message to his column on the other side of the river for them to cross as soon as possible. But the river was deep at that point. The water was filled with melting ice and cold enough to kill a man in five minutes. All the second column could use to cross was one leaky scow; on top of that, it began to rain.

Around noon, Middleton's forces failed in another attack, which even the support of the two Gatling guns didn't help. The cold April rain beat down harder than ever. For a while, the fight settled down to an exchange of rifle fire, broken here and there by futile charges by the Canadians. The militia fought well, but they were facing an enemy they couldn't see. They died in waves in the freezing mud. One of the Gatling guns went out of action and couldn't be fixed.

During the afternoon, the rain stopped and a watery sun appeared, giving no warmth. By now, some of the other column had managed to cross the river, but their crossing was slow and dangerous. Hardest of all was getting the horses across; and all the while, it was getting dark, with rain coming down again in great gray sheets.

By the time most of the second column had crossed the river, there was still enough light for a determined attack. Some of the Canadian officers argued, but Middleton refused to listen. He also refused to admit that he had been beaten. They were going to make a tactical retreat, he said. He became even more adamant when he saw a large column of mounted *métis* coming from Batoche to join the men in the ravine.

"We are going to pull back to Fish Creek," Middleton told his aide. "That is the order to be relayed to my Canadian subordinates. There will be no further discussion of the matter. We have a lot of wounded men, and they cannot be treated here, thanks to the wretched medical services provided by the Canadians. We had the men to take that ravine, but they didn't know how to do it. I doubt that the reinforcements coming from the east will do any better."

The British general laughed bitterly. "Ah, Winfield, if I only had some regulars—or a few *métis*. Say what you like about the half-castes, they know how to fight." His bitterness turned to sarcasm. "And do any of our Canadian friends know what has happened to the *Northcote*? We could turn that paddlewheeler into a gunboat—that is, if it ever arrives."

To convert the riverboat into a gunboat had been one of Middleton's first ideas when the campaign began. Built in 1874, the shallow-draught paddlewheeler had plied the South Saskatchewan in times of peace. It had two decks, with an exposed engine and boiler on the lower one, and a cabin and pilothouse above. On it, Middleton had placed thirty-five militiamen, a cannon, and a Gatling gun. The lower deck was fortified with a double wall of two-inch planks; the upper was protected by piled-up sacks of sand and grain.

Middleton's plan was to attack Batoche by land and by water. It was still a workable plan. But where was the *Northcote*? "I ask you, where is it?" Middleton grumbled. "What in blazes is causing the delay?"

Winfield did his best to explain. "The river is full of floating trees and sand bars. Even at full steam, the *Northcote* is slow. It's coming, sir."

"When? Next spring? Winfield, I want you to draft an order above my signature, using the strongest possible terms. I order the captain of the *Northcote* to proceed here with all dispatch. Never mind the snags and sand bars. I don't give a damn if he blows up the boilers. I want that infernal craft *here*! Send a rider downriver at once.

Now we will pull back to Fish Creek and wait."

"Looks like they're pulling out," Sundance reported to Dumont, handing him the telescope. Both men were concealed by heavy brush at the edge of the deep ravine. All along the ravine, the *métis* were spread out, waiting for the order to counterattack. Those closest to Dumont kept their eyes on their commander. It was raining again, a cold April rain. All day there had been nothing to eat but stringy jerked beef, with canteens of cold tea to wash it down. The *métis* fighters were cold and hungry. But the killing mood was still on them. A word from Dumont would send them swarming out after the retreating Canadians.

"If you go after them now," Sundance said, "You'll be fighting on the same ground they are."

"I know," Dumont agreed. "We could lose what we have gained. We will fall back and make ready to defend Batoche. They will not take Batoche, not even with that stupid steamboat they are bringing up the river. We will stop them at Batoche. It is then that I will ask Louis to offer his terms. It began at Duck Lake, but Batoche will be the place of decision. Our friend Hardesty will at last see some fighting."

After a forward party had been left behind in the ravine, the orderly retreat to Batoche began. The dead and wounded were brought home on sleighs. Compared to the Canadian losses, the *métis* losses were light; even so, many brave men had died defending the raw slash of earth that ran down to the river and continued on the other side. It was a somber procession that made its way back to Batoche.

Sundance and Dumont were among the last to leave the ravine. Looking back at it, Dumont remarked quietly, "This is called Fish Creek, but it is just a ravine. Yet so many men on both sides died here."

Some of the *métis* began to sing. "Listen to them," Dumont said wearily. "Most of them have lived along this river all their lives. They have stopped the great British general, and so they are happy and proud. They have reason to be. None has ever served in an army, none know of tactics. Farmers, trappers, fishermen, hunters—never soldiers—they have done what people said could not be done. Middleton's stupidity or caution helped, of course, but that is only part of it. They would have fought as well against a better general. But Middleton will come and continue to come, to advance like a great dead weight, a glacier. I hope my people will be able to go on singing. I do not sing myself, but I like to hear others."

That night, after Sundance and Dumont ate fried deer meat and oaten bread in the cabin, they went to the new meeting house to listen to Riel and the others. Hardesty and his Fenian subordinates were there, trim and warlike in contrast to the bearded, careless dressed *métis* commanders. The inside of the meeting house smelled strongly of raw pine and turpentine and tobacco smoke. Hardesty was holding forth when they came in. Hardesty nodded stiffly at Dumont and went on speaking, directing his arguments at Riel, who sat by the red-hot stove with a mug of steaming tea in front of him.

Hardesty was saying, "Louis, my friend, when I came here I thought it was to fight an all-out war. Instead, my men and I have forced to stand aside and listen to news of a lot of skirmishes, half-won battles. You beat them at Duck Lake, but instead of finishing them off, you chose to let them go. In the name of God, why? Where was the sense? Do you think they would have been as merciful? I think not. They would have hunted you down in the snow and killed every last man. You had them at Fort Carlton and Battleford. Once again, they were allowed to march away. Today, especially today, my men were held back again. For what reason? To defend Batoche was the reason given."

140

Hardesty paused to make his point. "I am ready to call it quits. I have had enough. With your permission, we will leave here as soon as we are ready. I have no more to say."

Riel answered him without standing up. "Don't be so hasty, my friend. Middleton and his forces are facing Batoche. Now is your time to fight."

"But why is Middleton facing Batoche, Louis? You said yourself he was defeated today. Why was your victory not followed up? Why are Middleton's forces still intact? Why aren't they scattered and broken, his men dead? If my men had been allowed to fight, there would not be a Canadian left alive. Instead, you are now forced to defend your most important town."

Riel looked at Dumont. "Do you want to answer him, Gabriel?"

Dumont nodded. "I know that some of my own people are turning against me because of the way I have been fighting this war."

From a number of *métis* commanders there was an angry murmur, and some of the faces that looked at Dumont were set in anger.

"Maybe they are right," Dumont continued. "For right or wrong, I was chosen as your general. From the beginning I never believed that we could win an all-out war against the Canadians. I still don't think it is possible."

A *métis* commander, named Thibault, a tall man with an eyepatch and a scarred face, shouted, "Then make way for a man with more courage. I have followed you faithfully, and so have my men, because we thought you knew how to command. But always, when victory was ours, you hung back at the last moment. What the Irishman says is true."

"Let him finish," Riel ordered without raising his voice.

Dumont said, "True. Everything Hardesty says is true. We could have slaughtered the Canadians at Duck Lake

141

and Fort Carlton. We could have killed every last man, cut the throats of the wounded. At Battleford we could have let the Indians scalp and torture and massacre the entire garrison—women and children, too."

"Mercy has no place in war," Hardesty said deliberately.

"Mercy didn't have much to do with it," Dumont went on. "If I thought a slaughter would guarantee freedom for our people, then I would soak this land in blood. I would spare no one, God forgive me, not the smallest Canadian child. I could go to my grave with that on my conscience if I had to. I didn't do it because I didn't think it would work. It has always been my plan to leave some opening, some middle ground where a bargain can be made."

Thibault's voice was heavy with sarcasm. "This is a fine time you have picked, with the British general only a day's march away. Is it part of your plan to let him take Batoche?"

Dumont said quietly, "My plan is to fight him at Batoche as we have never fought him before. Batoche has always been his objective. Batoche and nowhere else. If he fails to take Batoche, then he will know that his campaign has failed. That is why, if I am to remain your leader, we will stop him here. Stop him completely, fight him to a standstill. And when that is done, when he can fight no more, we will offer our terms to the Canadian government."

Hardesty stood up looking startled. He spoke to Riel. "I protest against this. Nothing was said to me about coming to terms. All along you talked of nothing short of complete independence. That was our understanding, and you gave your word on it. Do you think I have brought my men, some of them thousands of miles, to fight for half a cause? If all you wanted to do was discuss limited freedom, why didn't you get some of your French-Canadian friends to do it in Parliament?"

Riel refused to be baited. "You sound as if you would prefer war to any kind of peace."

"To the kind of peace Dumont seems to be talking about—peace without honor."

For a moment it seemed as if the debate would end in a killing. Gabriel Dumont's hand dropped to the hunting knife at his belt; his bearded face was twisted in sudden anger. "Are you saying I am without honor?"

Hardesty's thumb was ready to flip up the leather cover of his army holster. The other Irishmen were waiting to see how it went. "Your words speak for themself," Hardesty said, knowing that he had support from some of the *métis* leaders.

Riel got between the two men and ordered them to stop. "It would please Middleton and the Canadians if they could see you now. We are all men of honor. You, Hardesty, are so blinded by your hatred for the British that you can't see anything else. Maybe it will turn out that you have been right all along."

Hardesty said, "I know I'm right. They may accept your peace offer, but can you trust them? Once you lay down your arms, you will have nothing left to fight with, while they will still have their armies and their machine-guns. A peace made with a halfbreed rabble! Do you think they will honor such a peace? Yes, Louis, a halfbreed rabble! That's how they think of your people. I know, because that's how they think of *my* people—and they are the same color and live in the same islands. If my people are dirt to them, dirty, drunken, illiterate peasants, then what are yours?"

"I don't know," Riel said calmly. "Worse, I suppose. What would you do?"

Hardesty was no longer excited. His eyes narrowed and he spoke quietly, though his voice carried to every corner of the big room. "What would I do?" he repeated. "If I had been your commander from the beginning, I would have waged total war against the Canadians. There would have been no indecision. None! I would have made them feel the armed might of the *métis*. There would have been no talk of peace, not even a hint. Peace would come only when they had left our borders, when every one of their soldiers and surveyors and land speculators had gone. Armed might is all they understand. Make no mistake about it. How do you think the British—and the men who control Canada are British—built their Empire? By force. And by force it shall be torn down—not by peace offers or debates in Parliament."

Riel shook his head in wonder. "You would destroy the British Empire?"

"That will come, Louis, in a dozen small countries such as yours. Not now, but some day."

"But what about now, Hardesty?"

"It is still not too late to show them what you—we—are made of. Don't just fight Middleton to a standstill. Destroy him! Rouse up every *métis*, every Indian, who is not with you now. Let the English halfbreeds in Saskatchewan know that they must join our cause or be driven out. I would be ruthless toward our enemies and those who are waiting to see which side wins. After I destroy Middleton, I would turn the combined tribes against Prince Albert, the biggest Canadian stronghold in Saskatchewan, and burn it to the ground. With Prince Albert obliterated, its garrison wiped out, we would then control all of Saskatchewan except the towns in the south."

Dumont yelled, "The Canadians would still come!"

Hardesty nodded and continued to speak quietly. "They would. But I would make sure that, south of Batoche, they came into a country where nothing lived, where not a house or village stood. I would clear the land of livestock, burn every homestead, dynamite every bridge. South of Batoche, they would not find one scrawny chicken to make a pot of soup. Summer here lasts only weeks and winter comes quickly. By the time the first snow came, they would have had enough."

Some of the *métis* leaders murmured approval; others stared at the floor. Riel held up his hand. He spoke to Hardesty. "What you propose turns my blood cold, my friend. And yet... and yet. It may come to that if they refuse to meet our terms, or to offer terms of their own that we can accept."

Hardesty turned away but didn't leave. "Then all I've said hasn't meant anything. You're still ready to trust them after all I've said?"

"I'm ready to talk," Riel said. "I am ready to give Gabriel's plan a chance to work. And now, Gabriel, I am going to ask you a question, so there will be no misunderstanding later. What if they refuse to bargain?"

Gabriel Dumont's eyes were sad. "Then we will fight the Irishman's way." He looked directly at Riel. "Am I to continue as leader of the *métis*? If not, Thibault is a good fighter. And there is always the Irishman."

Dumont was so tall that Riel had to reach up to slap him on the shoulder. "You are still our general, Gabriel. So far you have led us well."

"I don't mind if you change your mind after I have left here. If there is any change, you will find me with my men."

Riel protested a little too strongly, Sundance thought, not at all sure that Riel wanted peace, no matter how much of it he talked. He was even less sure that Riel was determined enough to stand up to firebrands like Thibault.

There was silence as Dumont and Sundance left the room. The door had hardly closed behind them when voices were raised in loud argument.

The two men walked away, their shoulders hunched against the wind. "Listen to them" Dumont said without bitterness. "A few small victories and everyone wants to become the new general."

"What do you think?" Sundance asked.

"About what?"

"About Louis Riel? Will he turn against you?"

"Louis is my friend. I do not want to talk about it."

"All right, we won't talk about it," Sundance said. "I shouldn't have asked you."

Dumont said gruffly, "That's right. You shouldn't have asked me."

They walked in silence toward the barracks. The wind was very cold. Dumont stopped suddenly and looked at Sundance. "I don't know what to think about Louis," he said. "He is a good man, but . . . Hardesty knows where his weakness lies."

"It's still not too late to do something about Hardesty," Sundance said.

Seventeen

In the morning, the strengthening of Batoche's defenses began once it was light enough to see. Men wolfed down big breakfasts of fried meat and potatoes and mugs of scalding hot tea. For a while, it was quiet along the fog-shrouded river. Acrid wood smoke from cook fires mixing with the fog, as ice crackled in the river. Relieved after the long night's watch, stiff-legged sentries hurried to get a few hour's sleep before the work began again.

Dumont had worked during the night with a pencil on a rough map of the town and its approaches. Now it was morning, and he rubbed his eyes wearily while he speared chunks of hot ham swimming in raisin gravy and drank his third mug ot of tea. "We will dig more rifle pits and trenches," he said, "but not one behind the other the way it is usually done. The first line of trenches will be very shallow. If the Canadians capture them, there will not be much cover."

Dumont smiled grimly. "But before they capture anything they will have to get through the barbed wire—their own barbed wire. They left a lot of it behind when they surrendered Battleford. It was to be used to

147

fence off the land the surveyors decided did not rightfully belong to the *métis*. Have you ever seen it used in a war, Sundance?"

"Only in range wars. Usually, it was the wire that started them. No, I've never seen it used in a war. It hadn't come in yet while we were fighting the Confederates. It's one thing the Canadians won't be expecting. How do you figure to string it?"

"Not string it, Sundance. I though about that during the night. There is enough to roll it, using X-shaped supports. It will be rolled loosely but thickly. When it's rolled, it can't be cut, can't even be moved. The deeper a man gets into it, the more tangled and helpless he becomes. A brutal way to fight? It is. And there will be more surprises for the Canadians, especially for those on the steamboat."

Late the night before, they had discussed how the gunboat could be put out of action. It looked as if the plan would work. Dumont said it had to work, or the *Northcote*, sailing into the heart of Batoche, would play hell with its well-protected cannon.

Sundance was now thinking about the barbed wire. "They'll hang you for that, Gabriel," he said. "If they capture you, they will."

"Because it's against the rules of war? Do these rules really exist?"

"They claim they do. Both sides break them, but they're written down somewhere. They dust them off when it suits their purpose."

"There's a rope waiting for my anyway. It's been waiting since the first shot was fired at Duck Lake. I am not the brave man my people think I am. I think about that rope."

The work went on all through the day. Ax blades bit into tree trunks, and far into the night the circular saw in the steamdriven sawmill whined and snarled. Wagonloads of barbed wire were driven out past the first line of trenches and dumped in the mud; past there, the trees were cleared for three hundred yards. Whips cracked, and men cursed as the felled trees were dragged by teams of horses and piled one on top of the other in an impenetrable wall of defense that stretched from the high ground down to the edge of the river. On a knobby hill that dominated the road, more trenches and rifle pits were dug. One of the two Gatling guns was hauled up there by ten sweating *métis*.

"Don't drop that gun, you donkeys," Dumont roared, matching anxiously as the heavy rapid-fire gun was dragged up the steep slope. Five of Hardesty's Irishmen went up after it, carrying boxes of ammunition. During the day, another hundred Irishmen, looking hunted and tired, had arrived from the west, after having managed to evade the military patrols in Alberta. They had sailed from San Francisco to Seattle, then crossed the border into Canada from Washington state. They had hoped to follow the Canadian Pacific tracks into Saskatchewan but were forced to abandon the idea because military traffic was so heavy on the line. Instead, they had struck north into Alberta and headed due east toward Batoche. All Alberta, they reported, was up in arms.

"How do you like that?" Hardesty sneered at Dumont while the leaders were gathered around a fire for a late afternoon meal. "Does that sound as if they're getting ready to make peace."

Instead of answering, Dumont took his plate of food and walked away from the fire to sit on a tree stump some distance away. Sundance joined him, deciding he would never get used to drinking tea, no matter how strong it was brewed.

"What are you looking so gloomy for?" he asked Dumont. "The work here is going well. Even if they attack now, you are prepared. I can't say I ever saw a town as well defended as this."

Dumont chewed his meat without enjoyment. "I am

149

not worried about the town," he said. "I think Middleton can be stopped. I think they will fight harder this time. But that isn't what is on my mind."

"Then what?"

"I don't know. I have a bad feeling. I don't like the way Hardesty keeps talking to Louis. Every time I look, he is telling him something else. You are my friend, so I can speak plainly to you. This war seems to be affecting Louis more than I thought it would. I talk to him of one thing and he talks of another. One of the things he keeps coming back to is this church of his, this new Universal Church of North America. We are preparing for battle and he talks of a church. I talk to him of drafting a list of peace terms, but his concern is who shall be the pope of his church. He asked me if I thought Bishop LaFarge of Montreal might not be a good choice. Sundance, I don't even know who Bishop LaFarge is."

Sundance didn't know what to say.

"I am far from sure that the Canadians will even talk terms," Dumont continued. "It may well come down to the kind of war the Irishman wants so much. But Louis's mind seems to have gone beyond even that. You know what he asked me today? I was working with the men on the barbed wire and Louis walked all the way out there and called me aside. His face was pale and strained, and I though it was something important. Do you know what he wanted to talk about? He wanted to know what he should call himself when Saskatchewan becomes independent."

"What did you say?"

"If it hadn't been Louis, I would have thought he was joking. I was so surprised at first I didn't know what to say. 'I suppose president,' I said. We hope to be a free people with no allegiance to kings or queens, so I said president for want of a better word. Louis admires the French; they have a president. I thought that would satisfy him. But he shook his head and said that wouldn't do. All this time the men are waiting for me to get back to the wire. Louis then said perhaps 'protector' was a better title. He had other names written on a piece of paper; he didn't tell me what they were. He just walked away, still looking at the names on the paper. Later, I saw him talking to Hardesty; they were both looking at the list of names he had picked out for himself. Hardesty looked most interested, and they talked for a long time. It is possible that Hardesty added some grand-sounding titles to the list."

Sundance agreed that the Irishman was crafty enough to do just that—anything to get closer to the erratic man who held the fate of the *métis* in his hands. "But what does it matter what he calls himself?" he asked, knowing full well what Dumont was driving at but not wanting to put it into words. He knew the doubts that were going through the other man's mind. On the other hand, Dumont and Riel had been together for a very long time.

"If Louis's ideas become too grand, he won't be able to settle for a limited freedom," Dumont said. "Freedom within Canada won't be enough for him. My greatest hope is that the Canadians will agree to let him rule as governor of the *métis* province of Saskatchewan, our independence and land claims to be guaranteed by Ottawa as the rights of the other provinces are guaranteed."

"It sounds reasonable," Sundance said. "I can see the Canadians agreeing to that, even Macdonald, for all that he hates Louis Riel."

"Yes," Dumont said, "but will Louis agree even if Macdonald agrees?" He scraped out his plate without having finished all the food on it.

"You're not telling me everything, Gabriel."

Dumont looked at Sundance, then far out over the river, a grim gray in the gathering dusk. His dark eyes were as bleak as the icy river and the bare hills beyond.

"I think Louis is going to try to make it hard for the Canadians to talk peace."

"He's the leader; he doesn't have to talk at all."

"One side of him knows he has to talk, wants to talk. He would be going against everything he has ever said if he refuses to make the offer. Always, he has said that the Canadians forced this war on the *métis*. He is the peacemaker; *they* the warlike ones. Besides, our people do not want this war to continue. What do they care of governments or titles? As long as they can live freely in the old ways, they do not care who rules. They are simple people, but they are not stupid. No matter what Louis says, and they love him no less for his wild dreams, they know there will always be somebody in a frock coat who claims to rule them. The priest rules the village, and so on up the ladder to Ottawa. All my people ask is that their ruler's hand be light.

"But I think Louis wars against himself. Now, instead of drafting reasonable proposals, he is drawing up a list of personal grievances. That's right, Sundance, *personal* grievances. He has not talked to me of this, but I have been told that is what he is doing. He says the wrongs done him, including the years in exile, must be paid for with money. The sum in huge. The Canadians will certainly not accept that. That is why I think he does not want to talk."

"Then the war can only get worse."

"I know, and that is what worries me. It sickens me. It means that all this," Dumont waved his hand, "will come to nothing but more bloodshed. We have food now, but how long will it last? Hardesty talks of total war. Even if that fails, he can sneak back across the border and work his mischief somewhere else. Fools and rogues will always thrust more money upon him. Oh yes, Hardesty and his kind always manage to survive. But what of the *métis*?

Where can they run to?"

Suddenly, Dumont's face grew dark with fury. "I'll be damned to hell before I let my people die for nothing. I don't care if I have to . . ." He left the sentence unfinished and walked away.

Soon it was dark. Sundance went to Dumont's cabin; after lying on his bunk for an hour, he got up and cooked a solitary meal of steak and potatoes. There was some stale coffee, and he cooked that in one of the tea cannisters until it was as black as he could get it. The steak was thick and juicy; he didn't have to do much except singe it on both sides. It was warm in the cabin, and it was good to be in there with the wind buffeting the doors and windows. He ate slowly. It was an hour before he finished the last of the coffee, and still Dumont hadn't showed up. Sundance washed up and went back to his bunk.

Lying there with his hands clasped behind his head, he thought of all that had happened since he had left Chicago. So far he had accomplished nothing except to earn the friendship and trust of Gabriel Dumont. He realized there was nothing he could have done to prevent this war. Killing Louis Riel had never been an answer, even if he could have brought himself to kill the *métis* leader. There was something about the man that compelled respect, even when you knew he was more than a little crazy. All men that others followed blindly were like that. It had been a small war thus far, hardly a real war at all; there was still a chance it could be settled peacefully if Riel could be made to see reason. But as Dumont had pointed out, that wasn't going to be easy to do. When the time came, Sundance knew, there would be a split between those who wanted peace and those whose blood was hot for war.

Hardesty, of course, would be on the other side, and the Irishmen would follow where he led. Thibault would side with Hardesty. How many others? The ordinary *métis* soliders, the ones who dug the ditches and did the fighting and the dying, all looked up to Gabriel Dumont. Even so, there was Riel to be reckoned with. Even from an exile in Montana, he had maintained powerful grip on his people. The fact that he had been able to defy their priests, the center of their lives, and still maintain his popularity was proof of this. If it came to a showdown between Riel and Dumont, which man would the *métis* follow? It was hard to say. Riel appealed to their wild imaginations, but Dumont spoke in practical terms.

Sundance liked and admired Gabriel Dumont almost as much as he did General Crook. The two men were so different on the surface, but they had the same rough honesty, the same contempt for fancy phrases. Dumont and Crook were natural leaders; born fighters with no love of fighting. True, Dumont was a rebel, but so was Robert E. Lee, and there were few men with more honors than the old Confederate.

In the days to come, Sundance decided, Dumont was going to need all the help he could get. Hardesty was the man who was going to force the split in the *métis* ranks. As yet, there was no talk of the American expansionists coming into the war. They wouldn't try to grab Canada until the war got out of control. No doubt Hardesty was counting on that. There would be big rewards for the man who delivered such a rich prize into their hands.

The door banged open and Dumont came in, angry and tired. Sundance had a big steak waiting on the skillet; he put it on a bed of raked coal without saying a word. Dumont had a quart bottle of whiskey in his hand. He found two mugs and set the bottle down on the table. He filled both mugs and pushed one across the table to Sundance.

"Your steak'll be ready in a minute," Sundance said, tasting his whiskey.

"The hell with the steak," Dumont growled. He didn't

154

take the mug away from his mouth until it was empty. More whiskey splashed into the mug. It was gone in two swallows. "The hell with everything, my friend."

It wasn't the time to be talking temperance, Sundance knew, but he wondered where this drinking was going to lead. By his own word, Dumont was wild and dangerous when drunk.

"What happened?" Sundance asked.

Already Dumont had a wild look in his eyes. "Nothing much," he said, going at the whiskey again. "They were all there: Louis, Hardesty, Thibault, the others. I had to force Louis to agree to offer peace to the Canadians. You would have thought I wasn't there, the way they exchanged looks. When Louis saw how angry I was, he said, 'All right, my dear friend, Gabriel, my old comrade, we will try to make peace with them. We will do our best.' But he didn't hold out much hope. That's what Louis said."

Sundance didn't think it would do much good, but he dished up the steak and put it on the table. Dumont didn't even look at it. "I am tired," he said. "I have done my best for the *métis*, and for thanks I get strange looks." More whiskey slopped into the mug. "You know what I think I will do, my friend? I think I will take my rifle and my traps and ride far into the north. In my time, I have been in places few men have ever seen. I think I will go far into the Yukon, maybe to the mountains of Alaska. I can live out my life there."

"You can't do it, Gabriel. Everything will go to hell if you desert the *métis*."

Dumont yanked the hunting knife from his belt and stuck it in the table. "Desert! You call me a deserter? You are asking for your death, my friend." He finished another mug of raw whiskey. By now, the bottle was nearly empty. Dumont's eyes, red-rimmed from lack of sleep, glared across the table at Sundance, as if he didn't quite know

155

who he was. "Who are you to talk to me like that? I don't know you. Who are you?"

Dumont didn't want an answer. He finished the bottle and smashed it against the wall. His hand was close to the knife. "I don't like your face, you goddamned foreigner! You sit here drinking my whiskey, eating my food, and I see nothing but lies in your face."

Sundance's eyes were on the knife. "It's me, Sundance," he said, not wanting to fight the big man he liked so much. "I eat your food because I like your cooking. You fix the best ham and duck eggs in the North West."

"Duck eggs?" Dumont was puzzled, his eyelids getting heavy. "Duck eggs? You are talking like a fool. Or do you think I am a fool?"

"Never a fool, Gabriel."

"You're Sundance?"

"That's who I am."

"You saved my life."

"It was worth saving. Why don't you eat the steak? It's a good steak."

It was the wrong thing to say, and it made Dumont angry again. He picked up the steak and threw it in the fire. "I will eat when I have killed Hardesty and Thibault. No, I will drink."

Dumont lurched to his feet and picked up his rifle. He bolted a round into the chamber of the Lee-Medford and pointed the rifle at Sundance. "Get out of my way or I'll kill you," he threatened, swaying on his feet.

"You need another drink. I have a bottle in my warbag," Sundance said. "Over there."

When Dumont turned, Sundance drew his Colt and hit the big man across the back of the neck and caught him before he fell. The rifle clattered to the floor.

"You need some rest," Sundance said.

Eighteen

Gabriel Dumont groaned and opened his eyes as the good smell of strong tea and frying steak filled the cabin early the next morning. He closed his eyes and felt his head. Stooped in front of the fire, Sundance turned the steak with a fork. He filled a mug with bubbling hot tea, added brown sugar, and brought it over to Dumont's bunk.

Dumont took the mug and shouldered himself up on the pillows. "Thanks," he said, not wanting to look at Sundance. "My head...."

Sundance grinned at Dumont, who looked, for all the world, like a sick bear. "Drink your tea. The steak'll be cooked in a minute. If you don't want steak, I can fix ham and duck eggs."

Dumont drank the hot tea noisily. "I remember something about duck eggs."

"You wanted whiskey more than duck egges. That hurt my feelings, you hairy drunk."

Feeling the back of his neck, Dumont winced, then grinned with embarrassment. "You hit me, halfbreed. Thanks for hitting me."

"Don't mention it, friend," Sundance said, still

157

grinning. "Always glad to do a favor. You were mad and getting madder by the minute. In case you don't recall our little party last night, you were all set to kill Hardesty and Thibault. Can't say that I blame you. Still, I couldn't let you do it. You were drunk, and they might have killed you. You still planning to head for the Alaska mountains? You were fixing to become a hermit the last time we talked."

"Hurry up with that steak," Dumont complained. "One won't be enough."

When the first steak was half gone and the second one was frying, Dumont held out his mug and Sundance filled it with tea again. "I'd still like to kill the sons of bitches," he said. "I don't trust them, no matter what they say. How does it look out there?"

"Quiet. I was out at first light."

"I wish Middleton would attack. I'd like to get it over with." Reading Sundance's thoughts, Dumont said quickly, "I won't do any more drinking. Last night I though I'd go crazy if I didn't have a drink. I had my drink—my bottle—and I'm all right now. Did I . . . did I threaten to harm you?"

Instead of answering, Sundance took the second steak off the fire. "I don't see how any man can eat so much. You sure this will hold you for a while?"

"I'm a savage," Dumont said quietly, his eyes full of hurt. "To threaten a friend!"

"That's all right," Sundance said. "I'm a savage, too. When I drink I am."

"That doesn't make me feel any better."

"Eat the goddamned steak before it gets cold."

"I still don't know what to say."

"They don't say it. You know, Gabriel, you could get on my nerves if you tried a little harder. And by the way, general, you aren't fixing to stay in bed all day, are you?"

158

"Have some respect for a great leader," Dumont said, and they both laughed.

When they went outside, a group of men waved at them. Dumont yelled at them to come forward. One of them was scout from downriver. "The riverboat has arrived at Fish Creek," he said. "It got there this morning after sailing all night. Bugles are sounding everywhere."

"At last," Dumont said calmly. He called his leaders and told them what was happening. "The attack may come today. None of Middleton's men are on the move yet, but they will be moving soon. If they don't get here until late today, they won't attack until early tomorrow. That is my guess, but we won't count on it. They may hope to surprise us with a night attack. Double the scouts and strengthen the advance parties. All we can do now is wait."

Dumont and Sundance walked along the outermost line of defense. "Middleton has a thousand men," Dumont said. "We are half that number. This will be the first head-on battle we have fought. The next few days will decide how well courage and determination stands up against numbers and supplies. If we win, that will be just the start of our troubles."

Spirits were high in Middleton's camp. Well rested and well fed, the Canadian forces were eager to do battle with the *métis*. They had learned by their mistakes and had taken a measure of the enemy. Batoche, they swore, was not going to be like the other battles they had been through.

Encouraged, prodded by his aide, General Middleton was in a fighting mood. Winfield, young and ambitious, had hooked his wagon to the General's train. It would not do his career any good if they were defeated at Batoche.

He flattered the old man while hinting that a decisive victory was necessary for the sake of the General's reputation. For several years, Middleton had been talking vaguely of retirement, not to England but to the rich farmlands he owned in Ontario.

"A fitting conclusion to a great military career, sir," Winfield had said the night before. "You will be remembered in Canadian—Empire—history as the man who saved Saskatchewan, perhaps the entire North West, from savagery. You will be the man who wrote finis to Riel's monstrous career. After you have taken Batoche, sir...."

Middleton recognized the hint, the indirect threat conveyed by his aide. "Of course, Winfield, we will take Batoche. All that has gone before was merely preparation for the big battle ahead. Now we will strike quickly and decisively—supported by the *Northcote*. That's our trump card! We will batter down their defenses and take the town."

"I can see many rewards from a grateful government, sir," Winfield said blandly. "I can easily envisage a fine house built by popular subscription. The hero of Batoche! I can't see them doing less."

"Is that a fact, Winfield? Well, damn, why not? Lesser men have been rewarded for a lot less. And there will be a promotion and a decoration for you, my boy."

"Boldness, sir."

"Yes! Yes! Winfield. That's it, boldness!"

Early in the morning, Middleton's forces moved from Fish Creek toward Batoche. When the teamsters and scouts were included, his small army came to just over eleven-hundred men, supported by Gatling guns and cannon. There were six-hundred horses and thirty supply wagons. Signs of spring were everywhere; it was a beautiful day, sunny and fairly warm. The first spring crocuses were out, purple and yellow on the prairie.

The steamer *Northcote* moved north at the same time as the troops. Six miles from Fish Creek it tied up to complete its fortifications. Bags were filled with river sand and added to the upper deck of the makeshift gunboat. Extra ammunition and shells were loaded aboard for the Gatling gun and the cannon, as well as cordwood for the boiler. The Canadian force moved north again through thick brush, willows willows, and poplars. The trail followed by Middleton's force was hilly all the way from Fish Creek. As it neared Batoche it flattened out. There, Dumont added a line of rifle pits to the town's defenses that ran down to the bank of the river. They stretched south of the town for nearly a mile. Behind them was the main position, along the range of hills parallel to the valley. The slopes of the hills were thickly wooded and slashed by ravines. The rifle pits were four feet deep with breastworks of clay and logs. In the forward pits, two-hundred *métis* were positioned. Supporting them closer to the town were other *métis* and Hardesty's Irishforces. Hardesty had split his force; some were in the ravines, while others remained in the town.

All day long the *métis* knew exactly how far Middleton's force had progressed. Scouts reported back the General's every move. But they would have known even without the scouts, for the Canadian force was making no pretense of a surprise attack. Besides, it would have been futile to try to conceal eleven-hundred men and six-hundred horses, wagons, cannons, and machine-guns.

Just as Dumont had predicted, Middleton's army reached the outskirts of Batoche late in the day. The light was thickening fast, too late for an attack. The Canadian force camped for the night, out of range of the *métis* rifles, but the sound of bugles carried all the way into the center of the town. Both sides passed an uneasy night as they waited for the dark hours to drag on toward dawn.

In his tent, General Middleton turned a glass of brandy

and soda in his freckled hand and wondered what they would say about him in the London newspapers. The Atlantic cable had already flashed news of the rebellion to all parts of Europe. The French newspapers would attack him, of course, because the French could never forgive the British for having taken Canada. Damn the French! General Middleton decided. A bunch of jabbering, excitable foreigners who couldn't talk without waving their hands.

Louis Riel bent over a table in his cabin in Batoche; he was writing in his diary, the record of his life that he had kept for many years. "I have decided that I shall be known as Protector of my country after victory is assured and a government has been established. Government is not the correct word, for I shall be the sole ruler, and it is not fitting that I should preside over a quarrelsome assembly of men with differing opinions. I shall begin my rule by. . . ."

Hardesty, oiling and cleaning his revolver, stopped now and then to take a sip of whiskey. It was after midnight and he would go to bed soon. There was a slow drip of light spring rain outside his cabin. Soon, Hardesty thought, soon it will all begin to fall into place. He had left Ireland so many years before, had been all over the world, and had enjoyed small successes and endured small defeats. Now, for the first time, greatness, fame, and power were within his grasp. He loaded the revolver and spun the chamber. He would kill to keep from losing it.

"Indeed I would," Hardesty told himself quietly.

Sundance and Dumont were still talking; the supper dishes had long been cleared away. They lay in their bunks, the fire banked high. Dumont was smoking his short, cracked pipe.

"You know what you have to do, don't you, Gabriel?" Sundance said.

"About the peace offer?"

"If Hardesty and Thibault get in your way, you have to move them. If the talks don't get started with Middleton, they won't get started at all. If they do get started later, the only terms you'll get from the Canadians will be to surrender or be wiped out."

Dumont said, "I have been thinking about it. Louis has agreed to talk to Middleton."

"Middleton may have orders not to talk to Louis—about anything. If Macdonald is as angry as you say he is, somebody else will have to approach Middleton."

"But Louis is our leader. If there is a *métis* nation, Louis is its leader. No one else can talk to the Englishman—to the Canadians through the Englishman."

"And if they refuse to talk to him?"

"Then that finishes it. It would be an insult to the *métis* if they refuse."

"No," Sundance said. "You could talk for the *métis*."

Dumont stared at the ceiling, at the smoke curling up from his pipe. "That is foolish talk, Sundance. All my life I have been a buffalo hunter."

"For a buffalo hunter, you're a pretty good general. You could speak for the *métis*, as well as anybody else—better than anybody else. The *métis* look up to you."

"If the Canadians won't accept Louis, why should they accept me?" Dumont said. "I think they would rather hang me than talk to me. They won't forget Duck Lake or the other battles. Why would they deal with me?"

"I'm not saying they will, but it's more likely than they'll deal with Riel. You are the general in this war. You give the orders. You could have slaughtered the Canadians at Duck Lake, Fort Carlton, Battleford. Instead, you showed mercy and let them march away to safety. You held back the Indians at Battleford when they were ready to butcher every man, woman, and child. How can the Canadians not recognize those facts?'

Dumont sounded irritable. "All right! All right! I know what you're saying. You preach more than a priest. What I'm trying to tell you is that Louis must make the peace offer."

"And if he can't or won't or drags his feet? What then?"

"How the hell do I know? I already told you: no Louis, no peace offer."

"That's no answer, Gabriel. You have to take over, if necessary. I don't mean push Louis out. I know he's your friend and you love him. But this is one time you can't allow loyalty to get in the way."

"If Louis asks me to speak in his place, I will do it. Nothing else. I won't go behind his back."

Sundance said, "That's just fine. But what happens to the *métis*? You know Louis won't ask you to speak for him. You have to do it yourself—when and if the time comes. Look, I know how you feel, but there's no way out of it, unless you want Thibault or Hardesty to do the talking."

"Those dogs!"

"I know. You'd like to kill them. Fine! Kill them later, and I'll help you. This is one time when guns and knives won't help. Face it, Gabriel!"

"Face what?"

"Your responsibility to your people. The other night you were saying that men like Hardesty always manage to survive. That's true, and it's also true of you. Right now, you could go to the States and do just fine. Whatever you want to do: army scout, hunter, a guide for sportsmen. The rest of the *métis* aren't that lucky. If this war goes wrong for them, they could end up starving like the Indians. I'm talking about the *métis* who are left alive."

Dumont turned over on his side and stared at the wall. "I am sick of all this talk. No matter what I say, you keep at it. All these arguments, I am sick to death of them."

"If you don't want to listen, why don't you get drunk? You're good at getting drunk. I ought to know. I had to look at your drunken face and listen to your stupid talk. You can find a bottle if you put your mind to it. Ask one of the Irishmen."

Dumont swung his legs off the bed and stood up, his scarred fists swinging by his side. "I'm going to break your face," he said. "I'm going to break your face and then throw you out."

"Try it, buffalo hunter," Sundance said, getting up and bracing himself. He wasn't sure he could beat Dumont. The man had three inches and thirty pounds on him, but there was more to it than that. Dumont was a wild man, drunk or sober, when he was roused.

Suddenly Dumont began to laugh, a deep, heaving rumble that came from far down in his chest. His huge body shook convulsively and the laughing went on. He bent over to slap his thigh, fighting for breath.

"What the hell is so funny?" Sundance said sourly, though a grin was beginning to twist the corners of his mouth. "Suppose you tell me what's so goddamned funny."

"I don't know. I was ready to break your face when I suddenly thought of duck eggs."

"That's a hell of a thing to laugh at."

"You don't think it's funny? I do. For the rest of my life every time I think of you, I'm going to think of duck eggs."

Grinning now, Sundance said, "That's a hell of a way to be remembered. But I do admit I'm fond of ham and duck eggs."

Dumont went into another fit of laughter. When it passed, he looked at Sundance. "All right," he said. "I got mad at you because I knew you were right and I didn't want to face it. What do you think I should do?"

Sundance said, "If the Canadians—Middleton—

refuse to talk terms with Louis, then you have to take charge. That's What you have to do, even if Louis objects to it. You already know that Hardesty and Thibault will oppose you. They can be handled. But first you must talk to the *métis* you can trust. Be very sure of them before you do anything. If word gets out, Hardesty and Thibault may try to move first."

"It could come to killing."

"It could. Chances are it won't if you catch them surprise. Anyway, it has to be done. If and when you do talk to the Canadians, forget about Louis's list of proposals. You want peace with honor, a pardon for all the *métis*, a guarantee of your rights as free men. Other demands can be worked out later. What is important is to get them talking. But what comes first is a cease-fire, a truce, an armed truce. The *métis* will keep their arms until binding guarantees are given by the Ottawa government."

"God!" Dumont said. "Gabriel Dumont making demands on the Ottawa government! I'd be a lot happier if I had stayed with the buffalo. You think I ought to trim my beard and cut my hair?"

"No," Sundance said. "You wouldn't be the same."

"Maybe Louis will listen to reason," Dumont said. "In his way, he wants only the best for the *métis*. I would hate it if he thought I had turned against him."

"He'll thank you if real peace comes," Sundance said, not altogether believing it himself. "Anyway, the *métis* will be grateful."

"You'll stick with me through this, Sundance? I don't know if I could get through it without a friend. God! I hope a truce comes quickly."

Sundance said, "That's only a beginning. Then we have to make sure that nobody breaks it."

Nineteen

The attack began at 5:30 the next morning. This time, Middleton didn't come directly at the town. The river road was heavily defended with trenches and rifle pits. Middelton sent a small force by the road but took most of his men in a wide circuit out onto the prairie to come in against Batoche from the east.

Watching the movements of the Canadian troops through his telescope, Gabriel Dumont remarked, "So he's trying to play fox at last. It won't do him much good. It's a good thing the high ground to the east is defended. The Gatling gun on the knob will catch them when they start to come down the slopes. If we make it hot enough for him up there, maybe he'll fall back to the road."

It was a lovely spring day, with green grass sprouting and the willows and poplars budding into foliage. The sun was coming up bright and warm, and even the birds were singing. In the river, the last of the ice was being borne away on the current. There had been no contact between the two forces yet. Middleton's soldiers were still out of range, and the *métis* were under strict orders not to do any random shooting. For the moment, there was enough ammunition, but unlike the Canadians, the *métis* had no supply wagon to bring up more boxes of bullets from the rear.

Middleton's men spent the best part of an hour taking up their positions for the attack. At seven o'clock, the *Northcote*, armed to the teeth, began to sail upriver, tooting its steam whistle, the signal that the combined land and water assault was about to begin. As the *Northcote* steamed into range, a hail of lead was thrown at it from the trenches and rifle pits along the bank of the river; but the boiler and the guns were protected by the double wall of planks and sacks of grain and sand. The *métis* riflemen kept firing, but the *Northcote* sailed on as if nothing were happening.

Bugles sounded from the river road and from the high ground to the east. Immediately, the artillery opened fire, sending shells screaming into the barracks. For the moment, the town itself, which was mostly on the west bank of the river, was out of range. The Canadians attacking by the river road ran into furious fire and were driven back almost at once, while the troops charging down from the high ground were met by concentrated fire from the Gatling gun manned by Hardesty's Irishmen.

Peppered by rifle fire, the *Northcote* steamed forward until it reached the center of the town. The cannon and the Gatling gun on the upper deck opened fire at the same time. A shell tore away the side of a house and it began to burn, sending long streamers of oil smoke out over the river. Another shell blew a wagon and a team of horses to bits, while the Gatling gun, firing one thousand .58-caliber bullets a minute, raked the waterfront, chopping up everything in sight. The cannon continued to fire as fast as the gunners could drop in the shells. If the *Northcote* wasn't put out of action, Batoche would be burning in a very short time. The Gatling and the cannon kept on firing until the riverboat had sailed past the limits of the town.

Now the *Northcote* was turning to wreak more destruction as it steamed back through the town. The river was wide there, and the turn was effected quickly. Suddenly, a roar went up from the *métis* as the enormous steel cable of the ferry was raised aft of the boat. The Gatling gun opened fire at once on the wooden shack from which the winches were operated. The shack disintegrated under the rain of heavy caliber bullets, but the cable was up and the winch was locked in place.

A short distance downriver, the second cable was coming up out of the water. In the second shack, the men turning the winch were killed when the Gatling opened fire. The cable began to rattle back into the water and would have sunk to the bottom if three *métis* hadn't rushed forward. One was killed before reaching the shack; the other ran inside and worked the winch.

Every rifle along the river bank was concentrated at the Gatling gun. It was well protected, but the furious fire drove the gunner and his helper into cover. The Gatling started firing again, but the cable in the river was almost taut. Sounding its steam whistle furiously, the *Northcote* headed straight for the cable, hoping to break it. The boat struck the cable held firm and the upper deck, the guns, the two smoke stacks, and the mast were torn away and fell into the river. Screams rang out from the middle of the river as men were cut by the cable or crushed under falling timber. The *Northcote* had shown no mercy to the town of Batoche, and the *métis* riflemen along the shore were ruthless in their attack on the crippled steamboat spinning in the grip of the current. Soon it was past the town, still turning crazily. The *Northcote*'s short career as a gunboat was over.

All the *métis* who had manned the trenches and rifle pits along the river were moved back to meet the main attack from the high ground to the east. Up on the knob, the Gatling gun, manned by the Irishmen, was firing furiously. The attack from the road had failed, and Dumont called back half the men from behind the second line of defenses; when the Canadians regrouped and attacked again from the high ground, they were met by deadly, concentrated fire. They fought fiercely, but were slowly driven back.

"It's not going to be so easy," Dumont said to Sundance while they were sharing a canteen of water in a forward rifle pit. The Canadians had been driven back to the high ground, from where they kept up a steady round of sniping. "Middleton seems to be using his head at last—or somebody else's head. We're going to have to move the barbed wire as soon as it gets dark. If they come down that slope often enough, they're bound to break through just by numbers. They're fighting damned well today."

The day dragged on. Several hours passed. The only action was heavy sniping from the high ground. Then, at two o'clock, another attack was launched from the river by men brought down from the slopes. At the same time, there was another fierce attack from the high ground to the east. The Canadians came charging down the slope, firing as they came. Like the *métis*, they were armed with Lee-Medfords. The fire from the bolt-action British rifles was fast and steady. For the first time, they had fixed bayonets attached to their rifles, and the bright steel flashed in the rays of the sinking sun. It took everything the *métis* had to beat them back. When the retreat was over, the slope was dotted with corpses. Just before the sun went down, a Canadian officer came out with a flag of truce and asked to be allowed to remove the wounded.

Watching the stretcher bearers working on the slope, Gabriel Dumont said to Sundance, "I think these militiamen are turning into soldiers. Only a few weeks ago they were farmers and storekeepers, drilling once a week so they could smoke and spit and tell stories away from their wives. Now they are getting the feel of it. Some are even getting to like it. I am thinking there may be a night attack. They will break through if we don't move the wire."

It got dark very fast. Winter was just over; the nights were still long and cold. A wind came off the river. Far up on the slope, the campfires of the Canadians could be seen. Down in the *métis* camp, great iron pots of pea soup were bubbling. The *métis* campfires were protected by trimmed tree trunks buried upright in the ground, that prevented the men from being sniped at from above while they ate. After the men ate, they melted back into the darkness to listen for sounds of the enemy, to watch for an attack.

"What time do you figure to start on the wire?" Sundance asked. The ham he was eating was hot and well peppered. He decided he was getting tired of thick pea soup, the favorite food of the *métis*.

"Not long after the men have eaten," Dumont said. "The Canadians, too. The Canadians are tired after the long day. Maybe even their officers are tired and not so eager for night fighting. We will move the wire into the new position and hope we don't make too much noise."

"They have flares."

"I was thinking about the flares. It can't be helped. The wire must be moved. I don't think there will be any more attacks from the road, so we will move even more men from the positions there. It's taking a chance, I know. I don't think there is anything else we can do. If they overrun the defenses, they have the numbers to finish us."

At eight o'clock, Dumont and Sundance led a party of fifteen men out to the first line of defense on the river road. Another fifteen followed. The first party was to lift the X-shaped wooden supports, the second was to drag the coiled up wire. They all wore leather gloves as protection against the long, glittering barbs.

"There is no way to do it quickly," Dumont warned them. "The wire will dig into the ground, so we must take our time. Don't get nervous if flares go off overhead, because our support will open fire immediately. So will the Gatling gun on the knob. I hope they will not hear us, but I know they will. If they open fire and some of you are hit, the others are to keep going. This whole fight is changing. We can no longer be sure of beating the Canadians. All right now, we begin."

Like a long steel centipede, the line of barbed wire began to move in the semi-darkness. Here and there it twanged as the barbs caught on something, a tree stump or a clump of brush. Dumont urged them to be more cautious. "If we can get it into position without the Canadians knowing, they will destroy themselves on it when they attack. If a flare goes off, get down as fast as you can and don't move. From so far up, they may not see the wire. Move!"

It took a full thirty minutes to get the wire away from where it had been. Up where the Canadians were camped, it was quiet. *Métis* riflemen with bullets already in the chambers of their rifles watched the dark slope while Dumont, Sundance, and the thirty men slowly moved the wire. The men cursed softly as the barbs cut through their leather gloves. They stopped to rest, watching for flares, and then went on.

Soon, the long line of wire had been brought parallel to the bottom of the slope. Then it was stretched across the wide opening on the slope, through which the Canadians would have to attack, since the rest of the slope was slashed with fissures and jumbled with rocks.

Dumont whispered, "I would like to anchor it more securely with stakes, but it's all right. It's not something you can break through or jump over. Get down!"

A flare arced up into the night sky and exploded with a soft popping sound, bathing the slope in garish light.

Sundance and the others threw themselves down behind the wire while the *métis* opened fire. The flare hung suspended in the sky while the brief exchange of rifle fire went on. A second flare went up, and the shooting continued until it went out.

"I don't think they saw the wire," Dumont said. "Nobody was shooting at us. I don't think there's much else we can do now. If they want some night fighting, then let them come."

They were back in camp, behind one of the walls of logs that protected the fires. It was about ten o'clock, with many long hours to go until dawn. "You're right about the Canadians," Sundance said. "They are fighting better. It's all a matter of getting used to it. That's how it was in the Civil War. The Confederates sneered that the Union volunteers from the northern cities couldn't fight. They said they'd wet their pants at the sound of the first shot, and so on. And they were right at first. But a little later in the war, those city men showed them how wrong they were. How long do you think this will go on?"

"They're not beaten yet. There's no use trying to talk to them till they're good and tired. They'll think about talking when there are so many dead they'll have trouble getting them all buried. If they get mad enough, they may not talk at all. If that happens, if they decide to sit it out and wait for reinforcements to arrive from the south, we'll probably have to abandon the town. We don't have the strength to counterattack and destroy them. Now we better get some sleep."

Wrapped in blankets, Sundance and Dumont slept by the fire. It rained along about midnight, but the fire dried them quickly. At one o'clock, they walked the lines of defense where the sentries reported nothing unusual. One old *métis* with a sour sense of humor said, "All I can tell you for sure, Gabriel, is they're still up there. If you don't believe me, you can climb up there and look for yourself."

Dumont said he would take the old man's word for it. "You know how old that man is?" he asked Sundance while they continued their tour of inspection. "He admits to being sixty-five, but I know he's at least seventy. I hope I can let him die in his bed with his grandchildren gathered around him."

Then it was three o'clock, and it was still quiet. Dumont threw a twig in the fire. "I'm thinking there won't be any night attack after all, but I have a feeling—a feeling and nothing more—that they will come a little earlier than usual. Before it is completely light."

"Why do you think that?" Sundance asked, knowing that Dumont trusted his feelings as much as he did. They were both half Indian; there was no need to explain. If you examined your feelings too deeply, the meaning was lost.

Dumont smiled. "Two reasons. I feel it, and that's the most important. The second reason is this: Middelton attacked at five-thirty yesterday morning. Exactly first light, very exact. Now Middleton will want to do something different, something to surprise us. Of course, it's all stupid. He can't very well attack after first light, so he will attack before. In the end, it makes no difference. We'll be waiting for him. The camp will be very quiet when he comes, with all the lazy good-for-nothing *métis* snoring in their blankets."

At four o'clock, Dumont quietly roused every man in camp and issued whispered instructions. The fires had been allowed to die down a little. It was quiet up on the ridge, in the Canadian position.

"If I'm wrong, there is nothing lost," Dumont whispered to Sundance. "Ah, but if I'm right...."

At four-thirty, it was still dark, with just a tinge of gray light appearing in the eastern sky. Gripping their rifles, the lines of *métis* waited. It began two minutes after four-thirty. Three flares exploded over the camp, washing it in blinding white light. They were followed by a wild roar from hundreds of men as the Canadians began their charge from the top of the slope. They had moved one of their Gatling guns to a forward position. Its six rotating barrels began to spit out bullets at the rate of a thousand a minute. Down the long slope they came, firing fast. A boy carrying the Canadian flag faltered and died as a bullet struck him in the stomach. Another soldier was killed before he could pick up the fallen flag.

The bugler was blowing the charge, and the attackers came on bravely, straight into the concentrated *métis* fire. From the knob, the Irishmen kept the Gatling in constant action, firing as fast as bullets could be loaded into the hopper. Still the Canadians kept coming, stumbling over their dead and wounded as they swept down the slope. They didn't falter until they saw the wire. If they had been attacking by daylight, they would have seen it long before. The wire stopped them at last. The first wave of men ran right into it and were immediately entangled in its coils, fighting madly to break loose. All the time the *métis* kept up a steady fire. More flares went up, making it easy for them to kill the helpless Canadians. Now there was even time to aim, to shoot carefully.

The retreat was sounded and the Canadians began to fall back, all except those in the wire. The last of the flares sank to earth, trailing a yellow tail of fire. The light in the sky was getting better. Up on the forward slope, the Canadian Gatling covered the retreat as well as it could. For a while the Gatling on the knob and the Gatling on the slope fought a fierce duel. It ended when the Irish machine-gunner blew the crank and the receiver from the Canadian gun. Then he turned the barrel of the heavy gun and swept the slope from one side to the other, blasting everything that moved. Wounded men held up their hands, but he shot them to pieces with .58-caliber bullets. Men were still struggling in the barbed wire. He depressed the muzzle of the Gatling and chopped them to bits.

175

"My God!" Dumont cried, waving his arms at the Irishmen on the knob. "Cease firing! Cease firing!"

The Irish gunner didn't obey immediately. On the slope, a wounded man was helping another man even more badly wounded. They were hardly able to walk; both had lost their rifles. A burst from the Gatling on the knob nearly cut them in two. Then, finally, the Gatling was silent.

Dumont and Sundance walked back to the fire. "They won't attack again today," Dumont said. "I don't think they'll attack at all. My God! I am sick of this killing. It has to stop. You know, I didn't really feel it until they machine-gunned those men in the wire. They were like animals in a trap. No chance of escape, just waiting to be slaughtered. I hate the sound of those damned machine-guns. They turn the men behind them into machines."

It was dawn, with a thin rain beginning to fall. On the slope, blood and mud were mixed. The dead crumpled bodies had fallen in awkward positions. Smokeless powder still stank on the fresh morning breeze. Now that it was quiet again, birds began to sing in the trees. The bugle sounded from the top of the slope.

"They'll be wanting to fetch the dead and wounded," Dumont said. "They lost so many this morning. Let them come. While they're doing that, I want them to see what we're doing."

He yelled for one of his commanders, a burly young *métis* named Verrier. "Take a hundred men and move south on the river road. There is a small Canadian force still there, so watch for an ambush. Fight your way through if you have to. I want Middleton to know that there will be *métis* south of him."

Riel walked over to Dumont, followed by Hardesty. Rubbing his hands together, Riel looked very pleased. "Ah, what we have done here today, Gabriel! They are destroyed! They are destroyed! That wire—brilliant! Now they know the armed might of the *métis*. They will be finished when Verrier's men cut them off from the south. Look at them up there on the hill, dragging away their dead. They will all be dead if they attack again."

Dumont said quietly, "Some of our men are dead, too. Many are dead."

"They will be remembered, Gabriel. As long as the *métis* are a people, they will be remembered, these brave men."

"Too bad we can't just wipe them all out," said Hardesty, staring up at the Canadian stretcher bearers. "Did you see the way my boys got that bunch in the wire? Fish in a barrel! Yes, sir, it was a sight to behold. Damn! I'd like to take a crack at the sons of bitches."

Dumont jerked his head to one side. "There's the hill, Hardesty. Why don't you take your Irishmen and climb it? They still have one machine-gun in operation."

The Irishman laughed. "You can't make me mad today, Gabriel. They sent a British general and more than a thousand men against us, and we stopped them cold. Middleton and his goddamned gunboat! Look, my friend, we've had our differences, but that's all in the past. We're on the same side, remember? Our next job is to finish what they started. Wipe them out, every last man—including Middleton."

"You aren't forgetting anything, Hardesty?"

The Irishman put a puzzled look on his face. "I thought I included everything. Was there something else?"

"The peace offer. Louis said...."

"Oh, well now, Gabriel," Hardesty said quickly. "What was said the other night doesn't have much bearing on things as they are now. They're whipped, so there's no longer any need to talk. That's how it is in a war. The situation changes from day to day, sometimes from hour to hour."

Ignoring Hardesty, Dumont turned to Riel. "You gave

your word, Louis. Tell me to my face that you don't intend to keep it. Come on, Louis, I want to hear it from you."

"You don't understand these matters," Riel said. "The other night you were angry and talked of leaving the cause. I—we—could not afford to lose you. That is why I gave my word, to persuade you to stay. It was not a lie, Gabriel. I gave my word because it was in the best interests of the *métis*. You would want that too. Listen to me, old friend. If we show weakness now, our cause will fail. The Canadians respect only strength. We have shown them that we are strong. Let us go on from here to build a nation."

"Then there won't be any peace offer?" Dumont's voice was drained of emotion. "You gave your word. But it doesn't mean as much as a pile of dog dirt!"

"You are angry, Gabriel. You will understand later."

"I'm not angry, Louis. I'm sad over all the fine ideas gone bad. In the end, you're just another politician. How can you say that you're better than Macdonald?"

Riel remained calm, smiling. "I am not offended. What I do I do for my people. There will be no peace offer. When they have had enough they will come to *us*! I don't want to talk any more about it."

Turning away, Riel was stopped by the hard flat tone in Dumont's voice.

"Then I will make the peace offer," Dumont said. "I have no choice but to do it without you. Too many *métis* have died already, and many more will die useless deaths if this war goes on."

Riel said, "You don't know what you're saying, Gabriel. I am the leader of the *métis*. There can be no talks without me. And I say no! After all these years, are you now going against the will of your own people?"

"Only against your will, Louis, or what you think is

your will. What about you, Hardesty? What about your will?"

Hardesty's hand wasn't far from his gun. The Irishmen who weren't in the trenches and rifle pits crowded in close to him. So did Thibault and some of his dissident *métis*.

"We can't let you do it, Dumont," Hardesty said. "It's been decided that there won't be any peace talk. That settles it. You have to accept that fact—or get out now. You threatened to do it the other night. You can still do it. Good as you are, you're just one man. What's it going to be? You can't fight everybody."

Dumont raised his rifle until it was pointed at the Irishman's face. You're wrong, Irishman. There's a round in the chamber," he said. "All I have to do is squeeze the trigger. I don't have to fight everybody. Sundance!"

Sundance drew his long-barreled Colt in an easy motion. At the same time, the *métis* who supported Dumont took a firm grip on their guns. Dumont looked around. "You may have more supporters than I have, Hardesty, but I'm ready to take a chance. When the shooting stops, the Canadians can come down and kill the survivors."

Seconds ticked by. The only sound in the camp was the crackle of the fires and the wind. Hardesty looked sideways at Thibault, who was ready to start killing, no matter what the odds.

"You'll be first, Hardesty," Dumont warned.

Sundance cut in with: "And Thibault will be second. Who'd like to be third?"

No one moved. Then Riel walked away without a word. Hardesty stared at Dumont. "Go ahead, have your peace talk. My guess is they'll spit in your face. I'll tell you one thing for sure, Dumont. You'll be sorry for this."

"Let's go, Sundance," Dumont said.

Twenty

While the *métis* and the Irishmen watched, Dumont and Sundance placed wide planks on the barbed wire and crossed over to the other side. At the top of the slope, a Canadian officer waved them to come up. Sundance carried the white flag; both men were unarmed. The stretcher bearers, not yet finished with their grisly work, stopped to look at them as they climbed the hill. Two hours had passed since the attack, but the sweetish smell of death was still heavy on the morning air. The sun was warm in their faces as they went up the hill. It was a long climb. The only sound was the Gatling gun turning in its swivel. It made a quiet, racketing sound.

"I wish Hardesty would try to take this hill," Dumont said.

"Up or down it's bad," Sundance agreed. "Can your people hold them while we're up here?"

Dumont nodded. "I picked the best men. They will keep Hardesty and Thibault under control, but it won't be easy. I'll bet Hardesty is already spreading stories that I am trying to seize control of the movement from Louis. More and more, I know that Hardesty will have to be killed before he kills me. Somehow I always knew it would come to that. I knew it the first time I saw the man. Has that ever happened to you with a man you met for the first time?"

"A few times," Sundance answered. "The first feeling was the right one."

"Hardesty will gloat if Middleton sends us away," Dumont said. "I guess we can count on not being hanged this morning. These British make such a fuss about honor."

"I hope Middleton isn't any different. You know what you're going to say?"

"No, I don't."

"Just as well. It'll come to you."

A man's arm was lying on the slope, torn from his body by Gatling gunfire. The body had been taken away; the arm had fallen off the stretcher. They both looked at it and continued to climb. If it hadn't been for the stink of death and the six barrels of the Gatling watching them from the summit, it would have been a very nice day.

"I feel bad about Louis," Dumont said. "I know I am doing the right thing, the only thing, and I still feel bad. The look on his face when he walked away. I don't think I'll ever forget that look."

Sundance, not certain that some nervous militiaman might not open fire at any moment, wasn't too concerned about Louis Riel's hurt feelings. He felt naked without his weapons, but there was no other way. If the Canadians found even a knife in his boot, they would hang him from the nearest tree. That would be a hell of a way to end up after all he'd been through.

They were more than halfway to the top. Up above, the Canadian officer waved his sword until it glittered in the bright sunlight. "Keep coming and don't try anything," said the officer, who was very young, in a too-loud voice.

Dumont spat in the mud. "Damn puppy. Why in hell is he carrying a sword? Not a saber, a sword!"

"Be patient, Gabriel. If it works, you'll be the hero of your people—the one and only Gabriel Dumont."

"You can go to hell, too, Sundance. But you're right. I'd like to see the look on Hardesty's face. How long do you think it will be before we get an answer, supposing they agree to even discuss it?"

Sundance did some quick figuring. "All the telegraph lines to the towns north of here are down. The Indians cut the wire to Fort Albert. Middleton will have to send riders south to Regina or Fort Qu'Appelle or to some station on the railroad. The answer will come back over the wires as fast as they decide to send it. An hour, a day, a week. It all depends on Macdonald. At least the message won't be coming to him from Riel."

Dumont looked surprised. "Oh, but it will."

"No, Gabriel. The message will be sent to Macdonald from *you*. You are not a messenger. You are the man in charge. That has to be made clear. As far as Middleton and Macdonald are concerned, you are the new leader of the *métis*. That's how it has to be. I know you don't like it, but there is no other way. What you say has to come from no one but you. Anything you promise, you will back up. So don't promise too much. Middleton and Macdonald will not listen too closely if they think you have to run to Louis Riel to confirm every detail."

"Then I will be a traitor."

"Not a traitor, Gabriel. Middleton and Macdonald must *know* that they have to deal with no one but you. Sundance's voice became soft. "You have been the leader since the beginning."

The Canadian officer stepped forward after sheathing his sword. "If you have any weapons, you must give them up now. Do you have any weapons? All right, follow me. You can throw away that flag. It won't be needed."

The crew behind the Gatling gun stared at them with open hostility as they followed the young officer over the crest of the hill. The riflemen guarding the downslope all turned their heads. A few of them spat.

It looked as if more of Middleton's force was assembled at the top of the hill that stretched back to open prairie. Wagons and horses were drawn up. The dead were in three piles some distance from the three large army tents, where doctors were working furiously to save the wounded. There were pools of blood in front of the tents. An amputation saw rasped on bone as they went past the last tent. Far back from the top of the hill, men were gathered around a line of camp fires, looking cold and tired in spite of the warming spring sun.

"This way," the officer said, pointing to Middleton's elaborate tent, big as a cabin. "Take off your hats. Hats off, I said."

Sundance said, "It doesn't matter."

Dumont took off his battered wool hat and crushed it in one hand. Sundance was forced to grin. As a diplomat, Gabriel Dumont was a good buffalo hunter. "Step lively now," the Canadian officer said.

Inside, General Middleton, his aide Winfield, and two senior Canadian militia officers were waiting. It wasn't a cold day, but the charcoal brazier was burning. Middleton's port-wine face had blotches of white in it; the plate of food in front of him hadn't been touched.

Winfield bent over and whispered to the General, who looked up quickly. "Why isn't Riel here?"

Dumont said slowly, almost painfully, "I am the leader of the *métis* now. I am Gabriel Dumont."

All eyes were focused on the big buffalo hunter, his rough clothing, his scarred hands, the battered hat being turned nervously between them.

"So you are Dumont," Middleton said, not wanting to believe it. "You have caused us a considerable amount of trouble. I ask you again: Where is Riel?"

"Louis Riel is in camp. I have fought this war, and I will talk of peace."

Middleton tried for irony. "Peace! Is that what you

want? You haven't been behaving very peacefully, have you! What makes you think that we are prepared to listen to you. You are nothing but a scoundrel and a rebel. Are you aware that I could have you hanged right now? I don't mean later. I mean this instant!"

To press his point, Middleton banged his fist on the table.

"You could do that," Dumont said. "We are unarmed. We came unarmed under a flag of truce, and you can do anything you wish. As a British officer...."

The Englishman bristled. "So you want to be treated as an equal, is that it! Well, I'll be damned if I do that. You are not a soldier but a skulking rebel. Why should you be treated as a soldier?"

Sundance had remained silent all the time. Middleton turned his bluster toward him. "And who are you? You don't look like one of these people. I don't know *what* you look like, but you don't look like a *métis*."

Sundance gave his name. It didn't mean anything to any of them.

"He is my second in command," Dumont said.

Middleton sneered. "The cheek of these people. Second in command, indeed! Next this fellow will be calling himself general."

Middleton's aide whispered to him again. "All right! All right, Captain, I was about to come to that."

To Dumont he said, "Well, you're here, so I might as well listen to what you have to say—not that I'm going to give it much heed, mind you. Come on, out with it. Before you start, I might as well tell you that the only peace I'll consider is complete surrender."

"Then there is nothing to say," Dumont said. "We will not surrender, not if all your five-thousand reinforcements from the east were to arrive here today."

"Pretty well informed, aren't you?" Middleton said. "Very well, you won't surrender. You don't expect *us* to

184

surrender, do you? From the look of you, you're mad enough to demand anything. Oh, go away. We'll overrun your town in due time."

"Like you did this morning, General?" Dumont's voice was quiet; there was no sarcasm in it.

Middleton's red face grew a darker red. "You dare speak to me like that? All right, never mind. You did put on a good show, but you can't win. Don't you see that? Of course, you don't."

"But I do. I have always know that, even before this war began. A man does not have to be very smart to realize that one small people cannot win against vast forces."

"Then what the blazes are you trying to do? Get everybody killed? Do what I tell you, man. Surrender! If you know you can't win, what else can you do?"

Dumont took a deep breath and released it. "We will fight on until we are all dead, every man, woman, and child. Before we let our woman and children starve, we will kill them ourselves. We will kill them because we love them. But the men will fight on. We will become like wolves gone mad with desperation. There is nothing we will not do. You may take our lands, brand us as traitors, and then you may think it is safe to bring in your settlers and build new towns. But we will be there, deep in the woods, where even your Mounties won't find us. And we will strike at you without warning, in the dead of night, when you least expect."

Middleton's voice was a whisper. "You're a madman."

Dumont shook his head. "Maybe I am, but what I am saying is true. Before we're finished, we will turn Saskatchewan into a place of terror. You can send all the soldiers you like. You can hang and burn and flog. It won't stop us. In time, death will stop us. But death is a long time coming. I ask you this question, General Middleton: Is it worth it?"

"I'll be damned," the General said. "I've never heard such talk in my life, not even in Ireland. "Frankly, I don't know what to say. Tell me, man, are you really serious about all this fighting and killing?"

One of the Canadian officers answered instead. "He's serious, General. You can count on that as on nothing else in this world."

Middleton was still reluctant. "But I can't make deals with these people," he said to no one. "Anyway, it isn't up to me. I can't imagine what the Prime Minister will say if I forward such a message. 'Dear Prime Minister Macdonald, the *métis* government has offered to make peace with yours.' It's ludicrous. It's a political matter, and I want no part of it."

"Perhaps I'd better explain your position, General," Dumont went on, as if Middleton hadn't spoken. "Your men have fought bravely, but I think they have had enough of it. I know my people have. You still outnumber us, but soon you will be cut off from the south. A force of *métis* has already moved out. If the fighting continues, you will only lose more good men. Let me remind you, sir, that your men are not regular soldiers but volunteers, citizen soldiers, every man with a vote. Fathers, brothers, relatives with votes. The same is true of the men coming from the east."

"They will obey their officers."

"As long as it pleases them. If they find themselves bogged down in a hopeless war, you'll see how long they obey their officers. The French-Canadians don't want to fight at all. And then," Dumont's rough voice became soft, "you always have to consider the Indians, General. There are twenty-thousand Indians in the North West. The Crees and the Stoneys are already with us. So far, I have kept them under control. If they break loose, they will raid and burn from here to the Rocky Mountains."

"But that's unthinkable, man. What I mean is, you are

186

part white, aren't you? You couldn't turn loose the Indians."

"I can guarantee to control the Indians," Dumont stated. "I give you my word on that. If I cannot keep my word, I will give myself up to be hanged. Now, General Middleton, we have talked of many things but not of peace. I would like to talk of it now."

Middleton whispered to Winfield, who nodded and spoke to the young Canadian officer who had brought Dumont and Sundance to the tent. He nodded, too, pleased to be so close to the General.

"Come outside with me," he said briskly to Dumont and Sundance. They waited in the sunshine for about ten minutes. Then Winfield pushed the flap aside and put his head out.

"Bring them in, Parsons," he said, "then wait until you are called."

The young officer looked disappointed. "Very good, sir," he said.

General Middleton looked a little more confident when they reentered the tent. He was holding his large liver-spotted hands over the charcoal brazier and looked up. "I still don't know what the Prime Minister is going to make of all this," he began.

Winfield said smoothly, "I feel confident that he will see it as a wise decision on your part, sir. I'm sure the P.M. has no desire to become bogged down in a profitless and politically harmful war. But you were saying, sir...."

General Middleton was almost genial; he saw a new role for himself as a soldier-diplomat. "Now you must tell me what you want, Dumont. After you tell me, I'll try to sort it all out. If some of your demands are too outlandish, I simply won't relay them to Mr. Macdonald. I won't be made a fool of. Suppose you begin. Captain Winfield will make a list. You might as well know that he has already made a list of those frightful threats you made earlier. I

187

don't know how the Prime Minister is going to react to all that. Before you start, however, I must ask you if you are empowered to speak for the *métis*. I have it on good authority that Mr. Macdonald will have no dealings with Riel. If Riel is speaking through you, it's all a waste of time."

Dumont said, "I am my own man, General."

"Proceed."

Dumont's list was not very long. He used words sparingly and Captain Winfield was able to finish writing as soon as he finished a sentence.

"The rights of the *métis* to their ancestral lands, to be guaranteed by act of Parliament," Dumont said. "That lands taken from the *métis* be returned to them. That no new surveys of *métis* land be undertaken for any reason."

Dumont spoke for no more than twenty minutes. He could have finished sooner if he hadn't been so deliberate, so careful to make everything clear. When he said that was all, Middleton looked at him, as if seeing him for the first time.

"I am going to recommend that the Prime Minister... well, I'll be glad to see this damned war over with. As of now, a truce exists between our two forces. We won't be the ones to break it. See that your people don't. If they do, you can kiss your hopes goodbye. It'll be all over for you. Just one more thing. I am going to move my men back down to the river road. You'd better go ahead and give your people the lay of the land."

As Dumont and Sundance walked away with the young Canadian leading the way, the *métis* leader said, "It will be at least three days before we know. If we can only keep the peace until then. Think about it, Sundance. In three days, our people may be on their way back to their families, their farms. It's so close to the finish."

Walking silently, Sundance just nodded.

SUNDANCE: CANYON KILL LB618 $1.75
Jack Slade Western

Jim Sundance was the most expensive—and deadliest—hired gun in the West, but he wouldn't take on just any job. When Pete Duran wanted to prove that the Erskine herd hadn't been stolen by Comanches, but by Erskine himself, it was right up his alley. And it would take a bigger army than Erskine could hire to stop Sundance!

WHISPERING SMITH LB620 $1.75
Frank H. Spearman Western

The Crawling Stone Railroad was in trouble. Someone was sabotaging the tracks and trying to run the railroad out of business. Running down the men responsible would be a tough job, but if anyone could do it, it was the man called Whispering Smith. A classic Western story!

GUN HAWK LB621 $1.50
Leslie Ernenwein Western

Clay Payette looked mean, and he had a reputation for being a fast man with a gun, but he was a lawman, and he was honest. He was honest enough to be the only man General Shafter could trust—to become a spy! And Payette had to struggle with his conscience as well as a range war!

THE FEUD AT SLEEPY CAT LB611 $1.50
Nelson C. Nye Western

The town of Sleepy Cat wasn't healthy for Cross-Draw Boyd. When he wouldn't be chased out, someone tried to kill him, then framed him for murder. He was caught in the middle of a feud between the O'Reillys and the Pools, and the only way to safety was to settle the feud.

SUNDANCE: TAPS AT LITTLE BIG HORN
John Benteen

LB561DK $1.50
Western

Jim Sundance returns, and this time the half-English, half-Cheyenne hired killer is working without a fee. Some things are more important than money, and General Custer's threat to seize the sacred Black Hills is one of those. Only blood could redeem that insult— Custer's blood.

SUNDANCE: MANHUNT
John Benteen

LB562DK $1.50
Western

Another episode in the saga of Jim Sundance. He's not a man who enjoys killing strangers, but he's supporting a lawyer to help protect the interests of his Indian brothers, and you've got to be good at something to raise that kind of money — and Sundance is the best at tracking and killing men.

SUNDANCE:RUN FOR COVER
John Benteen

LB578DK $1.50
Western

The Sharps Fifty — a gun built to stop a ton of charging buffalo dead in its tracks. Someone was using it on the people of Bootstrap. He tried to use it on Jim Sundance, and that was a big mistake. If you wanted to live, you had to get Sundance with the first shot!

THUNDER RIDGE
Ben Thompson

LB580DK $1.50
Western

It was a hell of a mess. Mad Jack had finally put together the money to rescue his ranch, but the man who held the mortgage didn't want it paid off. To make it worse, they both wanted the same girl. This was a problem only guns could settle!

SUNDANCE: BLOOD ON THE PRAIRIE
John Benteen

LB577DK $1.50
Western

To the Sioux, two things were sacred above all—the Black Hills and the white buffalo. When a white buffalo appeared in the Black Hills, the tribes rejoiced, but if the Russian hunter killed the buffalo that joy would turn to war, and only Sundance could stop him!

RAMROD VENGEANCE
William Hopson

LB564ZK $1.25
Western

Some people don't like their jobs. They stay with them because they need a paycheck. Burt Howard was an engineer, not a cowhand, but for the paycheck he wanted he had to ramrod a ranch for a woman. His paycheck was revenge!

SUNDANCE: COMANCHEROS & RENEGADE
Jack Slade

LB569RK $2.25
Western

The half-breed hired gun comes up against his toughest opposition, a gang of deserters and desperadoes called the Comancheros, and they're so mean it takes two books for Jim Sundance to finish them off. A special Double Sundance!

WITH BLOOD IN THEIR EYES
Steven G. Lawrence

LB572ZK $1.25
Western

Halleran found the town turned into an armed camp, ready to start a war to keep the reservation away. It wasn't Halleran's issue, but he wanted to bring his brother's killer to justice, and that might be the spark to start the shooting!

SEND TO: LEISURE BOOKS
P.O. Box 270
Norwalk, Connecticut 06852

Please send me the following titles:

Quantity	Book Number	Price
_____	_____	_____
_____	_____	_____
_____	_____	_____
_____	_____	_____

In the event we are out of stock on any of your selections, please list alternate titles below.

_____	_____	_____
_____	_____	_____
_____	_____	_____
_____	_____	_____

Postage/Handling _____

I enclose..... _____

FOR U.S. ORDERS, add 50¢ for the first book and 10¢ for each additional book to cover cost of postage and handling. Buy five or more copies and we will pay for shipping. Sorry, no C.O.D.'s.

FOR ORDERS SENT OUTSIDE THE U.S.A.
Add $1.00 for the first book and 25¢ for each additional book. PAY BY foreign draft or money order drawn on a U.S. bank, payable in U.S. ($) dollars.
☐Please send me a free catalog.

NAME _____
(Please print)

ADDRESS _____

CITY _____ STATE_____ ZIP _____
Allow Four Weeks for Delivery